Critics Love

"Oh, ye of little faith, are

... Post

"It's powerful, visceral TV."

USA Today

"A brilliant piece of filmmaking . . . as smart as it is slick . . . strikes a nice balance between tough reality and an optimistic sensibility . . . all done with a bit of class."

New York Daily News

"It is genuinely uplifting in the best sense . . . first rate . . . revolutionary."

Washington Times

"It has a knack for plucking emotional chords that can touch even the most cynical viewer."

Knight-Ridder Wire Service

"Redemption is hard to come by, but *Angel* delivers the goods."

Dallas Morning News

"A remarkable television series."

Denver Catholic Register

"A delightful surprise . . . real in-your-face dialogue . . . the feel-good series of the season."

St. Petersburg Times

"The first time I watched *Touched by an Angel*, I left my friends, fell on my knees, and wept. Later I learned there had been no need to hide my feelings. My friends had been crying too."

Barbara Reynolds, *USA Today*

"Two years ago, I wrote about my divorce from network prime-time television due to irreconcilable differences. But one show has brought me back . . . *Touched by an Angel*. . . .it produced the most satisfying response I have felt while viewing a television program in many years."

Cal Thomas, *Los Angeles Times Syndicate*

"On TV, the unbelievable is routine. . . . But perhaps the most radical idea, at least by TV standards, comes from CBS's *Touched by an Angel*, which boldly insists each Saturday night that God does indeed exist."

Los Angeles Times

"Clearly, *Angel* has struck a chord with viewers, and in places you might not expect. . . . Its viewers cut across demographic, economic, religious, and racial lines. Letters come by the thousands. . . . The show continues to grow in the ratings with virtually no promotion from CBS."

Adweek

"*Touched by an Angel* is the kindest series on network TV. It may also be the boldest."

Star Tribune

"*Touched by an Angel* . . . isn't shy about plumbing the depths of pain and desperation of its weekly lead characters, precisely the people who need an angel most. It isn't shy, either, in speaking blatantly about God and prayer."

Newsday

"Beautifully shot and sharply written, it manages to confront real-world problems head-on, with a minimum of fudging or smarminess."

TV Guide

"Critics are being blown away by the frank spirituality and altogether solid storytelling of this very unsappy descendant of *Highway to Heaven* . . . a deep and savvy gut-level drama."

Fanfare

"There are several wonders surrounding this show: it is an unlikely hit that has reenergized Saturday night for CBS."

The New York Times

MARTHA WILLIAMSON
and ROBIN SHEETS

TOUCHED
BY AN
ANGEL

ZondervanPublishingHouse
Grand Rapids, Michigan

A Division of HarperCollinsPublishers

Touched by an Angel™
Copyright © 1997 by CBS Inc.

Requests for information should be addressed to:

📕 ZondervanPublishingHouse
Grand Rapids, Michigan 49530

Library of Congress Cataloging-in-Publication Data

Williamson, Martha.
      Touched by an angel : stories from the hit television series /
Martha Williamson and Robin Sheets.
      p.   cm.
    ISBN: 0-310-22159-5 (softcover)
    1. Fantastic fiction, American. 2. Angels—Fiction. I.
Sheets, Robin. II. Touched by an angel (Television program)
III. Title.
PS3573. I456286T6   1997
813'.54—dc21   96-49116
                                                        CIP

Interior design by Sherri L. Hoffman

Printed in the United States of America

98 99 00 01 02 03 /❖ OP/ 10 9 8 7 6 5

This book is dedicated to the Immortal
and Invisible star of *Touched by an Angel*
Almighty God
Wonderful Counselor
Everlasting Father
The Real Executive Producer

CONTENTS

ACKNOWLEDGMENTS

Special thanks to these people for their part in making this *Touched by an Angel* book a reality:

John Aiello
Loretta Barrett
Denise Ballew
Bob Colleary
Roma Downey
John Dye
Marcie Gold
Dick Guttman
Sonya Hodson
Amy Houston
Cliff Lipson
Beverly Magid
Thom Parham
Della Reese
Ann Spangler
Suzonne Stirling
Jennifer Toy
R. J. Visciglia

SPECIAL THANKS

*T*here would be no *Touched by an Angel* book if there had not been a *Touched by an Angel* television series, and there are many people responsible for that.

To CBS Television—to name only a few would risk omitting so many others. Suffice it to say that never have I seen so many network executives take such personal interest and pride in a family show. To everyone at CBS: assistants, executives, vice presidents, and presidents, past and present, my deepest appreciation for your sterling commitment to the little show that could. CBS is truly the Tiffany network.

To John Masius—creator of the original *Touched by an Angel* pilot. You explored a difficult realm and blazed the trail for us with a very personal story. And your legacy of Roma and Della has made all the difference. Thank you for so graciously rejoicing in our success.

ON LOCATION WITH
TOUCHED BY AN ANGEL

11

To Marcie Gold and Sonya Hodson—the true miracle of *Touched by an Angel* has been your friendship and unflagging commitment. Just when it all seemed hopeless, God sent you. And here we are. You are the real angels.

To R. J. Visciglia—the hardest working man in Hollywood. And Salt Lake. And Hollywood. And Salt Lake . . . "Let a smile be your umbrella."

To Dan Johnson and The Idea Institute—for your vision and generosity. God bless you.

To Marc Lichtman—my talented friend, our brilliant composer, the last "writer" on every episode.

To Jon Andersen—producer, director, friend, tribal elder. You've been there since Day One and you've gotten us all through every day since with humor and dedication and great, great spirit. For being this show's silent executive producer, thank you forever.

To the Staff and Crew of *Touched by an Angel*—no guest star leaves the *Angel* set without remarking that they have never worked with a finer, more dedicated crew than you. For your loyalty and long hours, many, many thanks. ✎

A WORD ABOUT THIS BOOK

*T*his book includes a collection of four episodes of *Touched by an Angel* which have actually aired on CBS television. They have been novelized from the original scripts by my friend and collaborator, Robin Sheets. Robin took on the daunting task of turning television dialogue and sketchy shorthand directions into short stories that capture the essence as well as the message of the show.

Credits appear before each story, identifying the writer or writers of the script's first draft and in some cases the writer whose initial idea or development of the story contributed to the final product.

However, there are many other writers and producers who, around "the table," contributed their talents to these and other *Angel* episodes. I would like to thank them all.

—M. W.

T was sitting on a cold, stainless steel table, barely covered by one of those cruel paper gowns that nurses point to just before they walk out of the examination room. I was thinking about my new job. After fifteen years working in television, I was finally the executive producer of a network show. The only problem was that I was producing *Touched by an Angel*—a title, by the way, that I found appalling.

The series had an order from CBS to produce only six episodes—hardly a show of confidence. The line on the show around town was that it was a "six and out," doomed to cancellation. All anyone knew about *Touched* was that the pilot had been scrapped and we were retooling. That's the showbiz euphemism for desperately starting all over again. At least we still had Roma Downey and Della Reese and the word *angel*. I had to hire an office staff, a writing

EXECUTIVE PRODUCER
MARTHA WILLIAMSON

staff, and a crew, reconceive the series, rework the characters, write a new premiere episode, cast it, find a director, and shoot it in Salt Lake City—in the next three and a half weeks. And then make five more immediately after that. The last place I wanted to be was sitting around naked wearing a piece of paper. But it was actually part of the job. So I occupied myself by looking out the window down onto Hollywood Boulevard.

I stared at the strange sculpture that some community agency, in a sad revitalization attempt, had recently chosen to grace the unofficial gateway to Hollywood: that being the corner of Hollywood and LaBrea, just half a block from Mann's (the former Grauman's) Chinese Theater and only a few seedy blocks from the now-terrifying intersection of Hollywood and Vine. The sculpture appeared to be of four apparently aluminum women—sort of Retro-Deco nudes forming kind of a steel gazebo, its neon canopy supported by their heads, topped off like a Christmas tree with a tiny statue of Marilyn Monroe.

Now, everything that happens in Hollywood starts with the pitch—the verbal presentation of the idea for a movie or a television series by a writer, producer, or executive. I tried to imagine what the pitch had been for that disturbing sculpture:

> "It's Southern California. It's the nineties. We're in a convertible turning onto one of the most famous streets in the world. We expect a portal of mythic triumph to lead us into this star-lined thoroughfare. We anticipate a tribute to eight golden decades of filmmaking and the men and women who made it all happen. Here, in the film capital of the universe, we want a landmark that says: 'Yes! Yes! You're in *Hollywood* now!' So, let's put four shiny statues of naked girls out on the corner, throw in some neon, stick

> Marilyn on top with her dress flying up in her face,
> and surround the whole thing with palm trees."

The first time I saw the new gateway to Hollywood, I was driving to a meeting at CBS Television City. I didn't think much of it at the time, since a block later I stopped at a red light and got caught in the crossfire between a fleeing suspect and the LAPD. Although I do remember thinking something along the lines of "Yes, yes, you're in Hollywood now!"

If there was any question before, there was no question in my mind now as I sat shivering in the doctor's office staring out the window: I didn't much like that silver statue thing down on the boulevard, especially now that I was at that moment just another barely clad woman in Hollywood wondering what she was doing there.

Finally, the door opened and a nurse stepped in. She whispered nervously, "Miss Williamson, we have a problem with Miss Reese."

I was alarmed. Della Reese was in the next room, getting her insurance physical. By coincidence, our appointments had been set at the same time, and now we were both being examined by one of those "showbiz doctors." These are physicians hired by insurance companies to confirm the health of stars and key executives before the beginning of a television show. If something was wrong with Della, my career as a key executive was suddenly looking very short. Show business insurance doctors are not famous for their comprehensive physicals, to say the least. If you are alive and standing in your gown, you have a very good chance of being approved for an eighty-hour workweek. Therefore, if these guys had concerns about a masterpiece of physical hardiness like Della, then something really must be wrong.

The nurse went on. "Miss Reese refuses to sign her insurance form."

My first thought was she didn't want to reveal her birth date, like so many actresses. But although I had only known Della a few days, she was clearly not the kind of woman to shrink from a straight answer. As far as I could tell, she was deeply proud of every day she'd spent on this earth so far and would be happy to tell you about any one of them if you asked. So this had to be a different problem.

The nurse went on. "In the blank where it says anticipated length of employment, I wrote six episodes. But Miss Reese won't sign it until I change it to say ten years. She says it's 'a God thing.'"

I looked back out the window at the naked women on Hollywood Boulevard and laughed out loud. Only a few days earlier, Della's star had been placed right outside on the Hollywood Walk of Fame. The lady had been around this town a lot longer than the aluminum girls or I had been. She had the faith. You don't make it in this town unless you're willing to stand out there, naked, and say, "I believe in myself." Della had done that. Many times over, I imagine. But today, she stood up in her little paper gown and said she believed in me, as well. And most importantly, she believed that God had brought us all together.

I turned to the nurse. "I guess you'd better change the form. If Della says ten years, then that's what we ought to plan on."

I went back to the corner of Hollywood and La Brea the other day and discovered upon close inspection—something I don't recommend—that the ugly metal caryatids were actually statues of former screen stars. And they were not nude at all, in fact, but just wearing really tight aluminum evening gowns. Fortunately, they weren't going to have to sit in them any time soon. It was a rather nostalgic visit for me. Three years had passed, but the silver girls and I were still standing. And so was *Touched by an Angel*.

The inscription over the Gates of Hell in Dante's *Divine Comedy* reads: "Abandon hope all ye that enter here." A lot of people think that might as well be the inscription above the gateway to Hollywood.

Don't believe it.

Martha Williamson
Los Angeles, California

PART ONE

THE MIRACLE OF
Touched by an Angel

MARTHA, ROMA, JOHN, AND DELLA ACCEPTING
AN AWARD FROM THE WEINGART FOUNDATION

CHAPTER 1

THE MIRACLE OF TOUCHED BY AN ANGEL

"It's the iffiest of all the new shows and could even be scuttled by the time you read this."

TV GUIDE, SEPTEMBER 21, 1994

That was the first of many death knells sounded for *Touched by an Angel* before it premiered in the fall of '94 on CBS. Most television critics considered the show to be dead on arrival. But viewers felt differently. Despite preemptions, erratic scheduling, and spotty promotion, the "little show that could" found its audience. And the audience just wouldn't let go. A year later, *TV Guide* congratulated *Angel* in its "Cheers and Jeers" section:

"And a seraphic flap of the wings to CBS, whose renewal of *Touched by an Angel* seems to have been a blessed event...."

TV Guide, September 2, 1995

Finally, in 1996, the "iffiest" of all the new network shows in '94, was graciously hailed by *TV Guide* as:

> ". . . CBS's family hit. . . . The most irresistibly loopy hour drama in a while, a show of many delights. . . . High style . . . beautifully shot and sharply written."
>
> *TV Guide*, January 13, 1996

I'm not exactly sure what the reviewer, James Kaplan, meant by "irresistibly loopy," but I liked it. It sounded like a lot of fun. And that's what *Touched by an Angel* has been. Tremendously gratifying, deeply challenging, an unqualified blessing . . . and a whole lotta fun.

More satisfying than earning the accolade "hit," is that critics don't refer to *Touched by an Angel* anymore as "the nearly canceled hour-long fantasy." Finally at home in our Sunday night time slot after *60 Minutes*, the show is now "the hit family drama."

I always considered the show to be a serious—if loopy—drama. The naysayers and pundits considered it a long-shot joke "without a prayer." But Roma Downey, Della Reese, John Dye, CBS, and the rest of us who have spent the last two or three years making *Touched by an Angel* now consider it nothing short of a miracle.

Perhaps the greatest miracle of all is that *Angel* has not only survived, but thrived as a drama that explores moral and spiritual choices, taking a definite and unapologetic point of view: God exists, God loves you, God wants to be part of your life.

It is a genuine and sincerely offered message of hope. And despite its sentimentality and emotional chord plucking, viewers recognize its sincerity, and they respond with deeply personal mail that we receive daily. Letter after letter recounts lives that have been more than entertained, but actually moved to positive emotional and spiritual action. Families have been reconciled, addictions confronted, betrayals forgiven.

Inspiring others to self-examination of the soul and spirit is the highest and best goal of television. And the constant flow of letters from people who have chosen to change, to forgive, even to live after watching our show have kept us all focused on that goal whenever the future looked dim.

There is a phenomenon that happens now when a stranger discovers that one of us works on the series. We call it the "Touched by an Angel Salute." Inevitably, they gasp, put a hand to the heart, and say, "Oh! That's the show that makes you cry."

It's a tough world out there, and it's getting tougher. Everybody's faxing and modeming and on-lining and Fedexing and downloading. If you don't like it, change the channel.

Press the button. "Escape, Transfer, Delete." You can tell anyone anything anywhere in a matter of seconds now. But it still takes the same amount of time that it always did to get to know someone, to mend a broken heart, to give birth to a child, to grieve the loss of a friend. Even in a world of change, some things just aren't going to change. And people's emotions are getting lost in the "in-between." People need to cry, but who has the time?

I remember the ten-year-old boy I met on an airplane who told me confidentially: "My whole family watches your angel show. My mom and my sisters and me, we watch it in the living room. My dad watches it in the den."

Dad didn't want anyone to see him cry. Like Holly Hunter, who in *Broadcast News* schedules her emotions between jogging and breakfast, viewers now look forward to "feeling" something on Sunday nights.

Maybe people love the show for the same reason the critics hated it. It makes you feel something you may have spent

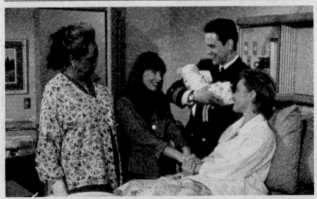

THE HAPPY ENDING OF "PORTRAIT OF MRS. CAMPBELL"

the whole week trying to suppress. It makes you cry. Or more accurately, it *lets* you cry. It asks you to consider that humbling yourself before your Creator and asking for advice is a sign of strength, not weakness. It suggests that in a world that demands so much of you every minute of every day, there is One who knows who you really are and loves you anyway.

That was the great truth I had to be reminded of before I could begin work on *Touched by an Angel*.

Due to the growing trend in spirituality and a revived fascination with angels, CBS had long been committed to doing a show about them. Indeed, a year before, even I had been asked to develop an angel show for the network. I wasn't the first to be asked, nor would I be the last. But their plans changed, and before I could pitch my rough ideas, they asked me to take on another, more pressing project instead: develop a woman in the workplace series.

I was relieved. My idea for an angel show was something along the lines of a Whoopi Goldberg-style angel in a pawn shop. And, after a tough couple of years in the romance department, I wasn't feeling very angelic anyway. I was much more at home writing cynical barbs for corporate women in a ten o'clock drama instead of spiritual eight o'clock family fare.

A year later, the angels came around again. On a Wednesday morning in May 1994 I was mourning CBS's failure to include *Under One Roof* on its fall schedule. Starring James Earl Jones, Joe Morton, and Vanessa Bell Calloway, the drama of an African-American family in Seattle was beautifully produced and directed by multi-Emmy-winning Thomas Carter. I had been brought in to help work out the kinks on the pilot and was set to run the show for Thomas if it made the fall schedule. It was a remarkable series that later did get picked up, thanks to Thomas's persistence and unshakable belief in its timeliness and quality.

But that day, there seemed to be no hope for the show. And worse, the CBS family slot had been filled instead by something called *Touched by an Angel*, previously titled *Angel's Attic*. The network sent over a videotape of the pilot that afternoon for me to view. The series had been picked up, but they were looking for a new executive producer.

The original premise was about an angel helping "Destiny's Tots." Roma Downey played a recently deceased human who was periodically sent to earth as an angel to watch over children whose destinies were threatened. Her current mission was to be a governess in a tract home in Los Angeles.

Tess was her cranky supervisor, the proprietor of a Victorian-style doll-house shop in Santa Monica, California. Tess clearly didn't like Monica, nor was Monica particularly happy to be working with Tess. Neither of them had much use for the Angel of Death, an ironic, jaded troll-like fellow (played by Michael J. Pollard). And God was something of an adversary, the corporate head of a company that nobody seemed too happy to be working for.

The story dealt mostly with the angry family's struggles to deal with their mentally challenged little girl. Though unable to get much response from the child, Monica got her attention with "magical" piano lessons and impressive special effects that stopped hurled objects in midair.

Near the end, the "Word" comes down that a member of the family must die before the rest of the family can appreciate their blessings. And so, the family dog is run over by a speeding car. Monica, breaking "the rules," raises the dog from the dead. The stunned family is reunited and they say good-bye to the mysterious Monica, never knowing that an angel has been in their midst.

In an interesting twist, the story also invented a previous life for Monica. As a turn-of-the-century human, Monica had been killed while saving her child from a runaway horse and carriage. Then, breaking "the rules" again, she visits her now-elderly daughter in a touching reunion.

The piece ends with a midnight visit from Monica to the autistic child. After a few words of encouragement, Monica elicits a few words from the delighted girl herself when the angel reveals her literal wings and elevates herself above the little girl's bed. To the child's delight, Monica spreads her computer-generated wings and flaps them up and down. Monica then flies out the window and back into the starry outer space universe from whence she came, back to "Angel's Attic," presumably where God, "that practical joker," resides.

In my opinion, the absolutely best part about the show was the potential of the stunning Roma Downey and the indomitable Della Reese. For all their screen combativeness, there survived an unmistakable chemistry that begged to be set free.

ROMA SHOWS OFF HER PITCHING ARM AS AN ASSISTANT BASEBALL COACH IN "SHOW ME THE WAY HOME"

Yet, as I watched the pilot, I sighed. I couldn't understand how this show could have been chosen over the elegant Carter series. And as a Christian, I just couldn't accept the concept of recycled angels who didn't seem to like God very much. So, in a childish, unconsidered fit of sour grapes, I called my friends at CBS Productions, Kelly Goode, Glenn Adilman, and then-president Andy Hill, and said thank you, but not interested. The show, though well intended, wasn't my cup of tea.

That precipitous move was the first of many lessons I have learned since *Touched by an Angel* came into my life.

Often, in *Touched*, Monica will ask someone, "Did you pray about this before you made your decision?" And her "assigned human" will admit to not having sought divine guidance.

I don't suppose many decisions in Hollywood are based on prayer. In fact, it's possibly professional suicide to admit that any business decision one makes in "this town" could be based on anything besides money and strategy. Money and strategy are, of course, very viable considerations. Ego, however, has contributed to more disastrous decisions in the entertainment industry than can be chronicled.

I'm ashamed to admit my decision to reject *Touched by an Angel* was made essentially on ego. I wanted to work on *Under One Roof*, a potentially award-winning class act. *Touched by an Angel*, if only by virtue of the fact that "soft" family shows are rarely so honored, wasn't going to garner much of anything except an early cancellation. The word was out on it already. Someone had slipped the pilot to certain members of the media, and once the bad buzz starts, it's impossible to turn around.

So, I had a sad luncheon the next week with Andy Hill and said good-bye to three years of a very happy association with CBS Productions. Andy, Kelly, and Glenn had been responsible for encouraging me and others to be the best writers we could be, to write from the heart, not simply "for" TV. Throughout the farewell meeting, however, I kept reminding Andy of things to consider as they revamped "that angel show." Even when the parking valet handed me my keys, I got in my car, rolled down the window, and made some suggestions as I drove away.

I prepared to accept a job on a courtroom series at another network. It would be the most lucrative position I'd ever held. But as negotiations dragged on, the memory of "that angel show" wouldn't go away. I kept thinking about it. I *cared* about it. And finally, I prayed about it. Albeit too late. Or so I thought.

I asked a friend to pray as well, and we both got the same answer: go back to CBS and try to get *Touched by an Angel* after all. But CBS was already considering other producers to take the job I had turned down. Worse, I would now have to inter-

view for the position I'd had in my hand only a week before. The deadline to accept my courtroom series was Friday. And I couldn't get back into CBS until the following Wednesday. What should I do? Take the sure thing? Or risk having no job at all?

There is a Scripture that I recall just about every time I walk into a

Hollywood party or a network meeting: "The Lord is my strength and my salvation. Whom then shall I fear?" I figured if doing the angel show was the right thing to do, then I had nothing to fear. Besides, what is it angels always say when they show up with news? "Fear not!" So, on Friday afternoon, I passed on the NBC drama series and settled in to wait out the four days until I could go back and try for the only other job on the horizon.

I walked into the meeting on Wednesday morning. There were lots of serious people in suits there, including former CBS Entertainment President Peter Tortorici. I cleared my throat and began my pitch.

I believed that people who would want to watch a show about angels wanted their angels to reflect a God who knew what He was doing. God can't make mistakes or change His mind. I told them that an angel show wasn't exactly my dream series, but if I was going to do it, I would put my heart into it. And that meant writing only what I could stand behind: that angels were messengers of God, not ends in themselves. The angels couldn't be fairies flapping their wings and granting wishes. God had to be Someone to reckon with. And at the end of each episode, the angels wouldn't win. God would. And we would, too, because people of faith are tired of being depicted on television as stereotypes, mass murderers, abusive parents, fanatics. I was convinced that a show that took spirituality seriously would attract an intelligent, rational audience of people for whom faith has a place in their lives.

I had the feeling I was speaking Latin. But I pressed on.

I explained that we had to ask the hard questions every week. "If God is good, then why did my baby die? Why did my marriage end? Where was God when I needed Him?" We had to meet head-on the inevitable criticism that faith is a cop-out to avoid dealing with reality, that belief in God is the opiate of the masses. Instead, I told them, faith is the most powerful weapon we have. And if audiences could turn off the television at night feeling inspired and empowered, they'd come back next week, and they'd bring more with them.

ROMA DURING HER FIRST ASSIGNMENT IN "SOUTHBOUND BUS"

I stopped to catch my breath. I'd gotten on a roll there for a minute. It crossed my mind that if this didn't work out, maybe I had a future in evangelism. But then I looked around the room. Silence. Nobody was yelling "Hallelujah."

More silence. Then the questions began.

Could I reshoot part of the pilot and make it work? I took a deep breath. "No." Wings? "No." Can they still be angels who used to be human? "No." Could we meet God? "No." Did I want to keep Della and Roma? Finally. Something I could say yes to.

"Absolutely." The incandescent Irish beauty of Roma Downey is nothing compared to her incomparably genuine quality. Her gift is sincerity. Della's is authority. Together they made the perfect team. And I couldn't wait to start writing for them. Already I could hear their dialogue in my head, the innocent and the sage.

They were very quiet, all those assorted presidents and vice presidents in the room. They thanked me and I left. I waited for a few nervous minutes in another office, and then Peter Tortorici walked in.

"Everything you just said in there. Go do it."

The next day I was sitting in a little office down in the basement of CBS. They gave me a phone and an assistant and a parking space that said "Ms. Williamson." It was the loneliest moment of my life.

I'd never been an executive producer before. I'd done just about everything else. I'd been a production assistant (read "go-fer"). I took the producer's dog to the vet, the Jaguar to the shop, the Armanis to the cleaners, and knew the Xerox repairman by name. I'd hauled cable as a grip for a film company, interviewed guests for a game show, supervised scripts for a Broadway musical, and typed musical variety scripts for three years on the last existing IBM Selectric in Los Angeles. I'd written jokes for comedians and patter for singers and copy for cable shows. I'd paid my dues as a sitcom writer and producer for six years, and two years earlier I had made the difficult crossover to drama. In fourteen years, I'd slept on couches in the editing room, and rewritten dialogue at three A.M. on skid row. I'd taken Drew Barrymore on Disneyland's Matterhorn ride three times during her dinner break. I'd reserved a suite for the Berosini Orangutans at Sportsman's Lodge. I'd been kissed by Placido Domingo and coached by Milton Berle. I'd taken meetings, done lunch, and been in development.

But even fourteen years in show business can't prepare you for your first call from an agent. I received thirty or forty of them on my first day as an executive producer. Agents for writers, agents for directors, agents for actors, agents for costume designers and makeup artists and directors of photography, etc. *Touched by an Angel* may have had only a six-episode order, but it was still work, and people wanted it. Bob Gros, the CBS head of production, walked into my office the next day and presented me with film veteran Jon Andersen. Jon would be the line producer on location in Utah. He would hire and supervise the "below the line" crew, and basically take the scripts and get them shot on time and on budget. More importantly, the quiet understanding was that Jon would make sure I didn't run the whole thing into the ground before we shot those six episodes and ended this doomed project. Jon told me later that when he moved into the Holiday Inn in Salt Lake City, he didn't unpack until episode seven.

A HARDWORKING CREW ON LOCATION IN UTAH

The first year of *Touched* went a lot like that. It was like doing guerrilla television. We shot in another state on a shoe-string budget. Those of us from L.A. lived on the third floor of the Holiday Inn and worked in makeshift production offices on the first floor. Jon doubled as the line producer, the unit production manager, the script consultant that first year. Ever-positive producer R. J. Visciglia did the post-production work of four people.

Two of my best friends became writers and producers—Bob Colleary, a very funny sitcom guy, and Marilyn Osborn, one of the few female action- adventure writers in the business. Not your typical choices for a spiritual family hour, but since I'd never been an executive producer before, it only made sense to hire a bunch of other people who didn't quite know what they were doing here, either. Sondra Latham, an assistant coordinator, was suddenly promoted to the crucial production coordinator position. She was a natural, and she's been the show "mom" ever since. Talented Nancy Cavallaro, a Utah resident who had been a wardrobe mistress, was now dubbed "designer." A construction fore-man, a visionary woman named Diane Millett, became the set designer. A brilliant still photographer, Karl Hermaan, was our director of photography, and an old college buddy of mine, musical genius Marc Lichtman, had never scored a television show but was now our composer.

From Utah we were blessed with the experienced sup-port of local Casting Director Cate Praggastis, Prop Master Bruce Wing, Locations Manager Lee Steadman, and Trans-portations Manager Larry Alexander.

Most of the film crew came from Utah. There were a few exceptions, of course, but it was hard to get experienced people from Hollywood to move to Salt Lake with only a four-month commitment. Despite the initial interest from agents, actually getting the experienced and sensitive directors we thought this show deserved wasn't easy. We took a chance on a former actor and proud Brooklyn bricklayer who had maybe four dramatic episodes under his belt. Tim Van Patten soon became a member of the family and helped shape the tone of the show as well as the warm atmosphere on the set.

We got the order to make two more episodes. Then, the order came for four more. It was hard keeping a crew together one week at a time, but it was an unusual crew. Salt Lake residents loved the show and were proud of its production quality and its family message. Most of them are still with us today, and we are all bound by those first uncertain months we spent together.

Della and Roma, of course, were instrumental in creating a wonderful feeling on the set. No day began without a hug and a great "Good morning, everybody!" from Della. Generous surprises of pizza and cookies from Roma kept everyone going on cold, late nights. They truly believed in the future of the show, and their enthusiasm was infectious.

We all realized we were doing something special one July day in the Utah desert. The temperature was 104 degrees, and we were shooting the first scene of the first episode where Tess promotes Monica to "caseworker." It was so unbearably hot, crew members were keeling over from dehydration. Finally, Della stepped away from the set and into the desert. She held out her hands to the sky and invoked the following prayer: "Lord, we need a cloud. And we need one now. Thank You, Father." She walked back to the cameras as if nothing had happened, but there was something about the confident way she had just ordered up the weather that made us feel that indeed, something was about to happen. Honest to God, fifteen minutes later, there wasn't just a cloud. There was cloud cover over the entire valley. The temperature dropped ten degrees, and we finished the day in the cool summer evening. The astonished crew stared at Della, who just shrugged. "It's a God thing." And she smiled.

While we shot in Utah, the writing staff in Los Angeles struggled to satisfy conflicting requests from CBS. Not to mention the writers' frustration as they watched my own efforts to conceive and develop a series while actually shooting it. There had only been three and a half weeks between my meeting with CBS and the first day of prepping the new "premiere episode" in July. It was November before the show really started to find itself.

Until then, there were the inevitable "creative discussions" with the network. "How," an executive asked, "could a piece of paper be blown across the desert and into Tess's convertible?" I thought of Della. "It's a God thing," I said. "God can do anything."

"If God can do anything," came the answer, "then why are there angels?"

I sighed. Good question. I came back with the only theology that works in a network bind like this: "Because you ordered six angel shows."

There were other creative discussions. For example, CBS wanted to know what was intended by the flight of the dove at the end of every episode. Was it God? Was it the Spirit of God? Was it something "religious"? I told them it was a nice way to put a signature on the series. A symbol of peace. They liked that. To paraphrase Freud, sometimes a dove is just a dove. Sadly, our first dove never got to episode six. Roma released him into the sky one day for an inspiring moment of symbolism and suddenly out of nowhere, a hawk symbolically swooped down and attacked him. Right there. On film. I hear that outtake is still making the rounds in editing rooms around Hollywood.

What with this being a show about angels and God and all, a Christmas episode didn't seem like much of a stretch. We got the story approved, although some of the guys in the corner offices weren't totally sold on a seventeen-year-old mentally challenged Southern boy whose best friend was a dying African-American six-year-old girl. But we pressed on, and created a beautiful tale based on Ken LaZebnik's single vision of an innocent bringing the good news of Christmas to a grieving congregation. It would be the first time that Monica would "fly" on the series—a special occasion, a necessary miracle. We were determined to make her flight not a special effect but an ascension, a breathtaking moment frozen in time. Something at once real and supernatural.

Everybody on the show was psyched for this. Despite very recent and painful back surgery, country music legend Randy Travis agreed to play the discouraged caregiver to his childlike brother. He would also record a Christmas carol for us. "O Little Town of Bethlehem" would play as the teenage boy, fearful of the dark, followed a Christmas star to the church at midnight. We had it all—snow, camels, lambs, donkeys, frankincense, mangers, flying angels, dying children, even members of the Gloriana and Mormon Tabernacle Choirs singing the entire "Hallelujah Chorus."

Then came "the call." Programming, trying to solve numerous problems of their own, wasn't sure anymore when the episode would actually air. Possibly January now. Could we take the "Christmas" out of the Christmas episode? Maybe make it a "Founder's Day" pageant instead?

RANDY TRAVIS WITH ROMA AND DELLA

There are days in your life when your entire career flashes before your eyes. Randy Travis was still in traction, the camel's agent wanted more money, Roma's "flying apparatus" didn't work unless she actually stood inside the manger to be elevated, and now . . . they wanted the Christmas out of the Christmas episode. I threw myself on the mercy of Executive Vice President Larry Sinitsky. Larry, not known publicly as a great sentimentalist, intervened and not only got us back on in December, but right smack on Christmas night. It was our highest rated show to date and has become sort of a "cult classic." Two and a half years later, we still get letters praising Tim Van Patten's stunning Nativity finale. The episode has repeated every Christmas since. Larry helped us that day and made me promise not to tell anybody that he could be a nice guy. Sorry, Larry.

The truth is, there were no bad guys trying to keep *Touched by an Angel* down by moving it around the schedule. They were, in fact, trying to find a home for it. If people don't watch a television show, advertisers won't pay to advertise on it. Keeping a show on the air that isn't being watched by enough people to satisfy the sponsors just isn't fiscally responsible. That's why it's show *business*. It's nothing personal. And yet, I was amazed at how many executives still took a personal interest in the show. I have on my wall a framed, hand-drawn parchment letter that Vice President Steve Warner fashioned for me himself. It reads:

> The Angel Formula: The angel meets her assigned human at a crossroads in his or her life. The angel (by the power of God) performs a miracle to bring that person to a point of decision or revelation. He or she, by their own free will, then takes life-changing action.

That was the premise for the show that we all finally agreed on. It hasn't changed.

By winter, we'd been preempted more times than we'd been on the air. When I mentioned that I worked on *Touched by an Angel*, people shook their heads apologetically and said things like "I'm sorry. I don't watch much TV." But *Touched* had become everybody's favorite underdog over at CBS Television City. Secretaries would call to tell me that this or that executive's wife loved the show. I've often wondered if we owed our first pickup in part to the influence of assistants and wives.

So we finished our first-year order for thirteen episodes and delivered some of our finest work that first season. Nevertheless, the future looked bleak. CBS gave us a last chance. They would put us on Saturday night for two weeks in a row at the end of February and the beginning of March right after *Dr. Quinn, Medicine Woman*. We had to prove that our loyal audience would follow us there and that we could pull better numbers on Saturday than in the suicide hour opposite the Wednesday night powerhouse hour of *Roseanne* and another ABC comedy.

Theoretically, all we could do was wait and see. Our offices were closed, and most people expected them to stay that way. But CBS production head Bob Gros had become a fan, and he refused to give up hope. "You are the vooman what must keep trying until the end is over," he would say urgently in his Dutch accent. "Dis angel show vill be back next year, and it vill be a real feather on your head." I learned long ago you don't argue with a man holding the checkbook. And so "The Dutchman" made it possible for us to keep our offices and phones going even after production had ended, just long enough to begin our "Save the Angels" campaign.

That's when God sent me two angels of my own, Sonya Dunn Hodson and Marcie Gold, two friends from a Hollywood professionals prayer group. They worked, without pay, for two months. They called every television and radio station and newspaper that would listen. And the ones that wouldn't listen got called back until they would. Soon, the production offices became campaign headquarters. They sent out tapes, they answered every fan letter, they set up interviews, they didn't take the word *no* seriously.

There was a time when the most exciting publicity we got was being Number 47 DOWN in the *L.A. Times* crossword puzzle: "Della of *Touched by an Angel*." But now, Sonya and Marcie had stirred things up. An editorial by Barbara Reynolds in *USA Today* made an emotional appeal: "CBS: Give TV's Angels a Break!" Articles were appearing in papers across the nation, and the network was receiving thousands of letters. When the "last" two episodes finally aired, *Touched by an Angel* met the ratings challenge. It was renewed for a second season and slated for Saturday night.

There have been lots of changes at CBS since then. Les Moonves left the helm of Warner Brothers to become the new CBS Entertainment President. He must have wondered why he inherited a borderline sentimental angel show that was 180 degrees from the sophisticated hip hits such as *ER* and *Friends* that he'd developed at Warner's. But Les stuck with us, too. And given the chance to really run, we took off. By the end of the second season, Saturday night had become "America's Night of Television." The next season, the angels moved to Angela Lansbury's prime Sunday night time slot after *60 Minutes*. And the angel-inspired spin-off drama *Promised Land* starring Gerald McRaney landed squarely on Tuesday nights against . . . who else? *Roseanne*. We consider that a good sign.

Somewhere in all the boxes of books I haven't unpacked since I moved three years ago, is an original paperback copy of the first *Star Trek* book. I bought it with my allowance when William Shatner was still wearing those V-neck collars. I devoured the whole history of who, what, where, and how the *Star Trek* phenomenon began. I remember to this day little details about the first year of the science fiction legend, trivia about the cast and crew, anecdotes about the wardrobe and the Tribbles.

What I remember most, though, was discovering that it took so many, many people to create one hour of my favorite television show. If you remember anything about this small volume, I hope that you remember the same thing. So many people gave their best to do something they believed in. Hundreds of people decided that *Touched by an Angel* mattered enough to work for, to fight for, to pray for. To all of them and to all of our viewers who have made it worthwhile, thank you.

—M. W.

PART TWO

THE STORIES OF

Touched by an Angel

CHAPTER 2

INTERVIEW WITH
AN ANGEL

Joe: "There is never a good reason for death."

Monica: "You don't know that until you die. How can you
judge something fairly when you don't even know the
rules? You can't play God, Joe. Because you aren't God."

The Story Behind the Story

*D*espite grim predictions, *Touched by an Angel*
returned to CBS in the fall of 1995. One of the
turning points in the campaign to keep the show
on the air came that spring when a full-page ad appeared in
Daily Variety. The headline announced that "God Is Alive and
Well in Hollywood!" The open letter to CBS implored the network to keep the show on the air, and it was sponsored and
signed by eighteen stars who had appeared in the first thirteen episodes.

The eternally optimistic Marion Ross, who passionately
led the open-letter campaign, was quoted at the bottom of
the article: "P.S. If Anne Rice can take out an ad for vampires,

God Is Alive and Well on American Network TV!
But for How Long?

CBS-TV is courageously bringing back the beautiful, inspirational, and, yes, even very entertaining *Touched by an Angel* series for a please-prove-to-us-that-the-audience-is-there four more shows.

If you long for emotionally fulfilling, provocative entertainment that confirms that faith is important in your life and in your TV diet, watch these shows AND GET OTHERS TO WATCH.

If enough of you find it in time, you will help continue a series in the inspirational tradition of *Little House on the Prairie*, *Highway to Heaven*, *The Waltons*, and *Dr. Quinn, Medicine Woman*.

Who are we and why have we contributed to this ad? We are the actors fortunate enough to have guested on this show and to have been "Touched by an Angel."

Brooke Adams	*Nia Peeples*
Nancy Allen	*Phylicia Rashad*
John Amos	*Marion Ross*
Elizabeth Ashley	*Susan Ruttan*
Obba Babatunde	*John Schneider*
Kevin Dobson	*Peter Scolari*
Gregory Harrison	*Randy Travis*
Ed Marinaro	*Dick Van Patten*
Rue McClanahan	*Malcolm-Jamal Warner*

P.S. If Anne Rice can take out an ad for vampires, we can take out an ad for angels!

Touched by an Angel returns Saturday, February 25
and Saturday, March 4 on CBS following
Dr. Quinn, Medicine Woman.

You Can Make the Difference

we can take out an ad for angels!" Her reference to Rice's famous trade paper promotion for *Interview with the Vampire* was the inspiration for our memorable season premiere episode: "Interview with an Angel," starring Gerald McRaney.

No two stories for *Touched by an Angel* are developed in the same way. Some are based on personal experience; others have been prompted by current events. Often, a story takes shape through the "Chinese Menu School of Writing." That is, we keep one list of interesting situations for Monica, Tess, and Andrew. On another list, there are compiled social issues and moral and ethical dilemmas. A bulletin board is reserved for clippings that writers tear out of the morning paper. Sometimes one angel situation from "Column A" plus one moral dilemma from "Column B" combined with a headline-inspired event from "Column C" will yield the multileveled story we are looking for. "Interview with an Angel" began like that.

We adopted the "interview" concept as a nod to Marion and all those who supported our return. It quickly became the obvious device for restating our premise and introducing our angels to our new Saturday night audience.

Soon, from "Column B," we added an idea we had been saving just in case there *was* a second season. Several months earlier, I had read in *Entertainment Weekly* the sad follow-up story of Jon-Erik Hexum, who died in 1984. Hexum, the star of the action-adventure series *Cover Up*, was fatally wounded when he held a prop gun to his head. Unaware that blanks could kill at such close range, he discharged the weapon. That horrifying story is probably recalled every time a gun is used on a set in Hollywood.

The *Entertainment Weekly* story, however, mentioned something I had not heard before. Hexum's family had allowed his organs to be donated. And one of them had been transplanted into a man who is currently in prison.

I read the story over the phone to Consulting Producer Marilyn Osborn. Formerly the vice president of development for Stephen J. Cannell and a writer from *The X-Files*, Marilyn was the first writer hired on *Touched by an Angel* and has been one of the show's best friends ever since. She and I agreed that this was the "forgiveness" story we had been looking for: "Does giving the gift of life automatically allow you to judge that life?" We tried numerous approaches to the story the first year, but finally gave up until the last piece of the puzzle fell into place at the last minute.

The writing staff was at the table one afternoon discussing our story. So far, we had a surgeon who must transplant a heart into the drunk driver who had killed the doctor's children five years earlier. But we had a practical problem. We had only seven days to shoot the show, and it all had to be shot in one location in Salt Lake City. How could we bring the scenes with the doctor and his wife into the hospital? Producer Glenn Berenbeim, our resident Renaissance Man, suggested that the wife could be a sculptor, installing a work of art in the lobby.

The first sculpture that came to mind was one I had seen only days before on Park City's main street. Park City is the ski town thirty minutes outside of Salt Lake. The heavy bronze sculpture brilliantly brought to life five exuberant children bundled up on a sled, joyfully coasting down a hill.

Suddenly, the whole story came together. The surgeon had lost five children who were on their way to go sledding, but never made it. The wife's sculpture was now a tribute to her lost family. Husband and wife would have to forgive each other as well as the man who killed their babies on a snowy day. And the journalist to whom Monica would relate this story would be the final "heart recipient." The actual Park City sculpture was even loaned to us for the show. It was one of the most difficult stories we ever put together, but one of the most gratifying, especially after we heard from the viewers. There is one letter in particular that none of us will forget.

After "Interview with an Angel" aired, we received a letter from a man whose chronic depression had convinced him that suicide was his only course of action. He had planned his death right down to the last detail: signing his organ donation card. But as he watched the season premiere of *Touched by an Angel*, something changed. Monica's words "You can't play God because you *aren't* God" affected him deeply. He described a spiritual experience, a sense of God's presence in the room. And so he chose to live. He sought counseling instead of escape. He wrote to thank us for that second season premiere.

And that letter belongs to everyone who worked so hard to make sure there *was* a second season.

—M. W.

INTERVIEW WITH AN ANGEL

TELEPLAY BY MARTHA WILLIAMSON
STORY BY MARILYN OSBORN
AND MARTHA WILLIAMSON

"An angel doesn't care about facts," Monica told the jaded reporter looking for a story about angels. "We're in the business of faith." Her account of a surgeon's struggle and the string of miracles that followed brought the reporter to her knees—before God.

"I sing because I'm happy!
And I sing because I'm free!
His eye is on even the little sparrow.
That's how I know he watches over me."

Tess finished her song, then turned to Monica and smiled. They looked down from their perch on top of the skyscraper to the busy street below.

Even an angel could get swept up in the energy that flowed through the streets of downtown Manhattan at noon. The people ran to and fro—everyone on their way to somewhere or something. Monica, a novice angel, was on her first assignment in New York City. Like any first-time visitor, Monica was awed by the giant skyscrapers, the masses of people, the honking horns and blaring boom boxes, and the smells emanating from corner delis and bakeries. "There are ten million stories in the naked city," Monica said. "And thirty million pigeons, I think. But I've never even seen a sparrow in Manhattan, Tess."

"Forget the sparrow," Tess said, frustrated. "It's a metaphor. You want to be any good at this job, you gotta stop being so literal."

"I know what a metaphor is." Monica reached into her pocket and pulled out a large artichoke. "This is a metaphor."

Tess frowned. "*That* is an artichoke."

Monica held it up to the light as if she were holding a precious stone. "I bought it in a market down there on the street. The little man told me it's got a heart inside that is so fragile and so delicious that it's worth all the trouble to get to it."

"What did I tell you about taking human form and starting in on the food?" Tess griped, taking the artichoke from Monica. "Now you stay away from little men and their metaphors."

"But you just said—"

"I know what I just said." Tess crossed her arms in front of her chest. "But sometimes I think you don't have the sense God gave a goat."

"You're not yourself today, Tess," Monica said, putting her arm around her supervisor. "Is something wrong?"

"Oh, I'm myself today all right," Tess replied. "Or at least a part of myself. But it may be a side you don't see too often. I love you dearly, Miss Wings, but this next assignment isn't like anything you've been asked to do before. If I'm not myself, it's because I'm not sure it's fair to ask, and I wonder if you're ready for something with this degree of difficulty."

Monica watched curiously as Tess opened what looked like a tabloid and riffled through the pages. When she got to the back section titled "Personals," she folded the tabloid in half, then once more. She pointed her brightly manicured index finger to a small boxed advertisement in the lower left-hand corner. With a few taps of her fingertip and the jingle-jangle of a wrist laden with copper bracelets, Tess had Monica on the edge of her seat. And it was a long way down.

There in bold eighteen-point type, sandwiched between a personal ad announcing "Passionate Adventurer Seeks Same" and another claiming "We Locate Deadbeat Dads" was the extraordinary ad: "Have You Seen an Angel? We Want to Hear from You. Call the *National Weekly* at 555-0126 and ask for Callie Martin."

Monica stared at the ad. "No, this can't be—"

"Oh yes, baby, this is it."

Monica took the paper from Tess and flipped through the pages. She'd never before seen headlines and photographs like those in the *National Weekly*. If they weren't so bizarre and tragic, she might have found them amusing. "Your mail is delivered by aliens," she read aloud, then turned the page. "Boy sees through his ears." Across the page was a snapshot of a boy with ears as big as an elephant's.

"Is this some kind of a prank, or a test to see if I'll really do it?" Monica asked. "Am I about to hear a chorus of angels engaged in a big belly laugh at my expense?"

"You know the fun and games come after an assignment is over." Tess wasn't smiling.

Monica turned again to the last page and reread Ms. Martin's ad. "This woman is looking for someone who claims to have seen an angel or met an angel. I don't think she'd know what to do with the real thing."

"You're probably right," Tess agreed. "But there are hundreds of journalists in the naked city. They need faith, too. Ms. Martin didn't have to run this ad. She could have just made up something about angels, like most of them do. But somewhere, down deep, she wants more. She wants to get to the truth." Tess rolled up the newspaper and used it to point toward a recently renovated office tower across the street, the headquarters of the *National Weekly*.

Monica eyed the rows of windows facing her. "Which one is it?" She would do her best to tackle this assignment with vigor and pluck—as always.

"There. Over six, down four."

Monica stopped just outside the open door of Callie Martin's office when she heard voices.

"I don't know what I was thinking the day I approved that one," a woman's voice said forcefully.

"We didn't get a lot of stuff, but what's here is pretty crazy," a male voice replied. "Here's a woman who says she's been channeling an angel named Fred for six years, and he just left her for a girl named Ethel." A pause. "Here's another good one. 'To whom it may concern, an angel changed my oil on the Taconic Parkway.'"

"But there's no proof," said the woman.

"Since when do we need proof?" came the reply.

"We're missing the hook here, Chris. You can get anybody to say they've seen a miracle. But if you can prove one, now *there's* a story."

Monica took a deep breath. It was now or never. She smoothed her peach skirt, straightened her straw hat, and tapped lightly on Callie's door. Then she stepped inside, clutching the rolled-up *Weekly* in her right hand.

"I'd like to answer your ad," she announced as she unrolled the newspaper and set it on the table in front of the brassy brunette in her early forties.

"Let me guess," the woman said in a bored tone. "You've had some kind of angel experience."

"I *am* an angel experience," Monica said. "I'm an angel."

The young man immediately stood up. "Of course. And it's great of you to stop by, but we just now decided we're axing the story—"

"Just a minute, Chris," Callie interrupted. "How long have you been an angel?" she asked, studying Monica.

"Forever," Monica replied.

"Well, let's narrow it down," Chris said. "Was it before or after you were captured by the Elvis clones?"

Monica ignored him and turned to Callie. "Let me tell you my story. By the time I'm finished, I promise you'll believe."

"What are you doing for lunch?" Callie asked.

"I heard about this great little place down on Fifth Street . . ." Monica began.

Chris's mouth fell open as Callie grabbed her coat and ushered Monica to the door.

"I'll be back in an hour, Chris," Callie said.

Monica had just stepped out into the hall and couldn't help overhearing Callie as she turned back around to grab the tape recorder Chris held out to her. "This is the hook we're looking for," she hissed. "A real nut."

"I need facts," Callie said as she and Monica settled into a corner booth at Gabriel's, a restaurant a few blocks down from the offices of the *National Weekly*. Their meeting seemed

CALLIE (DINAH MANOFF) INTERVIEWS AN ANGEL

to be typical noontime fare for Callie, but Monica found it unique and delightful, as she was seldom taken to lunch and particularly relished the earthly joys of freshly baked bread, steamed vegetables, and gourmet coffee.

Monica was delighted when she saw Tess, dressed as a waitress, approaching their table. After handing each of them a menu, she recited the daily specials, recommended the pecan-crusted trout, and wrote their orders down on a pad. Then Tess was gone, but Monica appreciated it when she kept reappearing. It meant everything was proceeding well, but that she should keep on her best behavior just the same.

"I want evidence with this story," Callie said as she pushed a button on her tape recorder. "I can always find a nearsighted bumpkin who went out for a walk and thought he saw something in the sky. But I need evidence. Something my readers can see. Let's start with your full name and address."

"My name is Monica and I live . . . everywhere."

Callie sighed and pushed the button on the tape recorder again. "I need some solid proof for this story. Like wings, for example. Do you have any wings you carry around with you or something? Could I touch the feathers myself? How about a halo?"

Callie delivered the sarcastic questions at a rapid pace, almost as if she didn't want answers, just Monica's reaction.

"Now, I've never understood this one," she went on. "Musical talent. Were you born with it or made to take lessons at some pearly-gated music academy?"

"Ms. Martin, I understand that you want proof," Monica said patiently, "but angels and proof don't have much in common. You'd probably never hear the two words in the same sentence. Angels aren't about proof. We're about faith. Faith is the evidence of things not seen."

Callie rolled her eyes. Then she looked straight at Monica. "Faith doesn't sell, my dear. I need evidence, something the readers can see." She sat up a little straighter. "Okay, why don't you just start talking, and we'll see where it goes?" She turned on the tape recorder again and sat back in the booth.

Monica cleared her throat. "Well," she said, with her perfect enunciation and Irish burr, "I'm Monica, and I've always been an angel. But I've only been a caseworker for about a year, which isn't long when you consider the scope of eternity and all—"

"Wait," Callie interrupted. "A caseworker?"

"Oh, I started out in the choir like everybody else, but then I went on to Special Appearances like, well, 'Behold!' and so forth." She felt herself shift into high gear now, as she rambled on about the details of her heavenly existence. "That didn't last too long because I got a transfer to Search and Rescue, which was very exciting, like *zoom!* push the train back, and *zoom!* get out before they see you. I spent centuries doing little bits and pieces of lifesaving, but never anything like casework. Tess—she's my supervisor but also my friend—she said I was just made for casework. Saving lives has its merit, but saving souls, and families, and futures, well there's nothing like it. You humans would say it's a 'rush' or something but—"

"Stop!" Callie looked totally confused. "Casework? Saving souls? Time out." A waiter delivered Callie's coffee, and she tore open three packs of sugar, grabbed a spoon, and stirred the brew with vigor.

Monica picked up the bottle of Heinz 57 sauce and studied it. "Ever wonder why some food is free and some food you have to pay for?"

"Huh?" Callie frowned and cocked her head, as if trying to figure out which planet Monica had stepped off of this morning. "You were saying something about casework. Describe a typical case to me."

Monica felt uncomfortable sharing the details of past assignments with this stranger. Casework was confidential. Still, a woman like Callie wouldn't settle for anything less than the facts. And Tess was expecting her to guide the reporter to a belief in angels and to help her find her faith in God. Ms. Martin would need some specific details; she was just that kind of person.

Monica decided it was time to trust her judgment. She would share the story of Dr. Joe Pachorek, a father of five, who had learned a lesson in compassion and forgiveness that had changed his life forever. Monica's role in the situation had left no doubt in Joe's mind as to the reality of angelic beings. If this story didn't convince Ms. Martin, nothing would.

It had all started the afternoon she and Tess sat down on a boulder to watch an excited group of young climbers unpack equipment, untangle ropes, and start up a mountain slope. Tess had pointed to a particular young man named Andy, the third in a line of seven climbers.

"At first I thought Andy was my assignment," Monica told Callie. "That's the first lesson. Assume nothing."

Monica and Tess watched as the group of seven, including Andy's wife of four months, scaled the steep mountain wall. They could hear Andy laughing and yelling back and forth to his companions. He was unhooked, free climbing.

"Come on, you guys. You're gonna kick yourselves if you don't—"

"Andy Grossman, live and unhooked," his wife called up to him.

Andy was obviously an experienced climber. No one seemed concerned that he wasn't attached to the others. Then, about fifty feet up, Andy reached his left foot out carefully for a toehold.

The next minute he was tumbling through the air. Monica and Tess watched in horror as his body bounced onto the rocks below. His wife's screams echoed throughout the canyon as everyone scrambled back down the mountain. Still, Andy lay there in the rocky dirt for over thirty minutes before one of the climbers finally reached him.

Monica was in the emergency room when Andy was rushed in on a stretcher. Tess had stayed behind to ride in the front of the ambulance beside Andrew, the driver, who was also an angel of death and colleague of Tess and Monica's. As Monica paced back and forth, waiting for word, she thought her job would be either to aid in the young man's miraculous recovery or to assist his family as they came to terms with his death.

An EKG was run immediately, and no activity was evident. Blood had stopped flowing to the young man's brain. But Andy's heart was still beating steadily, and so he was quickly hooked up to a ventilator and intravenous tubes. A staff doctor and emergency room nurse told his family he would make an ideal organ donor. The nurse found a donor card in his wallet, and a release form was prepared for his family to sign.

The time of death was listed as 2:42 P.M. The entire traumatic event had taken place in less than two hours.

Across town, Dr. Joe Pachorek, cardiothoracic surgeon, had just cleaned up after eighteen holes of golf and was waiting in line for a drink at the country club's poolside bar.

"No, it's just like holding a filet." Joe was explaining heart transplant surgery to an older man in line behind him. "You can't think of it as anything but meat."

Joe's wife Lisa stood beside him, her face expressionless. He knew she didn't think anything he said or did was funny. Not anymore.

The charity event had started with a golf game and would continue with cocktails, dinner, and an auction. Lisa was an artist, and one of her sculptures was on the auction block. Joe hadn't seen the piece; he actually had little interest in her work. Their marriage had been strained for several years now, and while they still lived together at the same address, they led largely separate lives.

Joe felt his beeper vibrating and reached for it. The hospital, of course.

"Excuse me," he said to the man and, ignoring Lisa, he made his way across the room to the phone.

"We need you right away . . . three hours ago . . . a transplant . . ."

A young man had died in an accident, and his heart and other vital organs were still viable. Joe couldn't hide his excitement as he returned to his wife. In twenty years of practicing medicine, the thrill of performing a delicate transplant hadn't worn off.

Joe looked at his watch. "Gotta go," he said and reached his hand out for the car keys.

She already held them in her hand. Her blue eyes revealed nothing as she gave them to him without a word.

She'd get a ride home with someone, he told himself as he hurried out to his car. She was good at taking care of herself.

Monica's role had evolved into coordinating the organ donation process for the hospital. She and Andy's wife were reviewing some forms when Dr. Pachorek blew through the emergency room doors and rushed past where they sat in the lounge.

Andy's young wife obviously felt overwhelmed with all of the decisions suddenly thrust into her lap, and she was having a difficult time coping.

"He signed his donor card just last week," she choked out between sobs. "He's always thinking of everybody else. He was—he's not dead, really, is he?"

"He's only being kept alive by machines," Monica said softly.

"But maybe if we waited—he could wake up in a month or so, couldn't he? I mean, miracles happen, don't they?"

"Yes, they do," Monica reassured her. "But Andy's death can save many other lives, and that's a miracle, too."

Out of the corner of one eye, Monica watched Dr. Pachorek as the attending physician explained Andy's condition to him.

"We'll have the paperwork completed soon, so you should be prepped for surgery tonight. The recipient is a thirty-year-old male. Only Stage Two, but he's been waiting for a match for two years. And this one's perfect. He's at the end—this is his last shot. The guy shouldn't have gotten this far. Guess he hit the second-chance express."

Joe motioned toward Monica and Andy's wife, then whispered something to the other doctor. The doctor nodded, and Dr. Pachorek took a few long strides to stand before them.

"Excuse me." He pulled at a few loose strands of grayish black hair on one side of his head. "I'm Dr. Pachorek. I'm the surgeon overseeing the procedure."

Andy's wife nodded numbly.

"I just want you to know that we'll treat your husband with the great care and respect he deserves," he reassured her.

She reached out to grab his hand. "Let them know . . . the ones that . . . just tell them how much we love him. He had . . . a very good, kind heart."

"I promise," Dr. Pachorek replied.

He seemed moved by her pain, but then he straightened and looked at Monica. She nodded, then stood and followed Dr. Pachorek over to the receiving desk.

"I'm the transplant liaison," she told him.

"I've never seen you before," he said, looking pre-occupied.

"Well, the committee likes to rotate supervisors, keeps us objective. I'm glad we've found such a perfect match for you."

"Great. So . . ."

"Monica."

"So, Monica, this kid's organs can go bad on me any minute, and I've got a recipient arriving any time now who isn't going to see next Tuesday if those papers aren't signed."

"Certainly, Doctor. She just needs a little time. She's in shock. When people experience sudden loss—"

"I know. Just do it, okay?"

They turned toward the set of double doors then as an ambulance pulled up and a gurney was wheeled in. Monica was surprised to see how young the recipient was. A Y-shaped scar framed his right eye and jutted down his cheek. She still believed her work revolved around the young couple, but she had already considered that the intended recipient might need an angel's strength as well.

Monica hurried back over to Andy's wife to finish helping her with the paperwork while Dr. Pachorek went over the recipient's chart with a nurse.

"It's been a long haul for Ethan," said a young man who had followed the gurney into the hospital. "He deserves a little good news."

At the mention of the name "Ethan," Monica watched Dr. Pachorek tense and flip to the top of the chart.

"Ethan Thomas Parker," he read aloud. His face was flushed as he slapped the chart down on the desk and snapped the top back on an expensive black pen. "Get yourself another surgeon," he said, and marched off the floor.

The attending physician looked helpless for a moment, then turned to the small crowd gathered around him. "Ethan Parker murdered Dr. Pachorek's children," he told them.

The noontime crowd at Gabriel's was thinning as Monica began to detail the tragic car accident that had taken the lives of the Pachorek children.

"Wait a minute, wait a minute," Callie stopped her. "A surgeon refuses to do a transplant on the guy who murdered his children. How come I've never heard about this?" She pulled a small cellular phone from her purse and punched in a number.

"That's Parker, Ethan," she blurted at Chris a moment later. "Find whatever you can, and get back to me at Gabriel's immediately. So you're eating? Just do it." She dropped the phone back in her purse and turned to Monica. "You should be the one getting me the background on this. There had to have been some news clips or a lawsuit—something."

"You're welcome to check out any of the facts, Ms. Martin," Monica replied kindly. "I'd encourage you to, actually. Just remember that I said up front, the business of an angel is faith, not facts."

Monica, so intent on telling her story, had barely noticed until now the steamed artichoke on the plate in front of her. Three small ramekins of various sauces had been placed at her elbow.

"There's drawn butter, yogurt, and white wine sauce," the familiar voice spoke. Tess peeled off the lunch check and handed it to Callie, then turned to Monica. "You'd better take a breath and eat your lunch, young lady."

"Thank you, yes, I will," she told her advisor. "Good food is such a great perk with this job."

"Don't get used to it," Tess replied, rolling her eyes as she strolled away from the booth.

Suddenly, the door to Gabriel's flew open, and Chris looked wildly around the room. When he spotted his editor's table, he pushed his hair out of his eyes with one hand, and with the other folded his pair of black Wayfarer sunglasses and hung them on the breast pocket of a heavily starched denim shirt. All the while he shuffled a large manila envelope from one hand to the other.

"Ethan Thomas Parker," he reported proudly as he neared their table. "Served two and a half years for running up a curb and killing five children in front of the Pachoreks' home."

Callie gave Monica a sharp glance. "Okay. Tell the rest of the story," she said.

Joe walked briskly from the emergency area and crossed the campus to an adjoining medical tower where he took the elevator up to the fourth floor. Once inside his office, he crossed the room to stare out over the campus at the emergency room where his children's murderer waited for the transplant that would save his life. He shook his head. There was no way. To save the life of the man responsible for the deaths of his children exceeded any Hippocratic oath he had ever vowed to uphold. No one would blame him if he returned to the golf course right now and never looked back.

He walked over to his desk and picked up the gold-framed photograph—his five children smiled up at him, their faces aglow with the spirit of Christmas. The girls wore red velvet dresses and plaid ribbons in their uniformly blond hair. The boys were dressed in green sweaters and bow ties that matched the girls' ribbons. The baby, Mary Ann, was just two years old. Neil, the oldest at nine and a half, proudly held Pickles, the family's cocker spaniel, in his lap.

Joe gently laid the photograph facedown on his desk and rubbed his forehead with a thumb and forefinger for several seconds. The memory of that fateful day came rushing into his mind like a whirlwind, and he couldn't stop it.

It was three years ago and the winter's first snowfall. The children had been pestering their father to turn off his basketball game and take them to try out their new sled.

"Daddy, come on, please . . . please Daddy." Sylvie pulled on his arm.

"We want to ride the new sled," Tony cried, his eyes bright with anticipation. At only three years old, this was his first real experience with the snow. He'd been too young last year to remember.

"Take us, Daddy," Clayton pleaded.

"Okay, okay . . ." Joe waved a hand at them. "It'll be over in just a minute."

"You already said that a long time ago," one of the children complained. All of their voices were beginning to blur together.

"I'm coming! Just hold on for one minute."

Joe could hear their pleas in his head to this day. He would start to get up from the recliner when one of the players would make a pass that would propel him back down in front of the television set. Funny—if you asked him today, he couldn't even tell you who was playing.

Lisa had finally appeared in the den and offered to take the kids herself.

"They're in overtime," he told her. "It can't be that much longer. Ten minutes, tops."

"That's forever to these guys. They've been waiting for this since Christmas. You've had twenty-four games since then. There's been only one snow."

Joe remembered slowly getting to his feet, his eyes still glued to the set. "Okay, I'm leaving. I'm getting up . . . Foul? Awww . . ."

"We'll be back in a couple of hours," Lisa said, leaning over to kiss him on the cheek. "We'll be over at the park."

Joe had to admit he was relieved when she fished a set of keys from her purse and told the children to go meet her in the car. With cheers of delight, they ran out of the room, Neil, Sylvie, Clayton, and Tony, in their hats, mittens, and brightly colored parkas. Mary Ann stopped at Joe's chair to kiss her hand and then touch it to his face. He grabbed her hand and gave it a mushy kiss, never taking his eyes off the set. Then she ran after her brothers and sisters.

Joe had just heard the back door slam when what seemed like a thousand different noises exploded into his mind all at once—the squeal of the tires, Lisa's screams, glass breaking, and the clamor of metal on metal. A child's terrified cry for help—that was the worst.

A drunken Ethan Parker had crashed his pickup into the children as they were piling into the family's station wagon. He was arrested at the scene and pleaded no contest to charges of involuntary manslaughter. He was incarcerated a few months later and served a two-year sentence in a minimum security facility.

In a matter of moments Joe and Lisa had lost every one of their children. Lisa had witnessed the entire scene, and while it was three years ago, the couple had yet to begin the healing process.

The pressure in Joe's head had increased to what seemed like a hundredfold in the few moments he'd stood by his desk remembering. He walked back to the window where the afternoon sunset was almost blinding. He was fumbling for the curtain cord when he caught sight of Lisa on the ground below.

She was standing beside a mover's truck and pointing, obviously giving directions to the two men who were unloading a wooden crate off the lift. Joe looked toward where Lisa was pointing—the recently completed annex to the hospital, an atrium, they all called it, because of its skylights.

The new space was the result of months of fund-raising, and the interior build-out was almost finished. Most of the hospital staff had watched the construction progress and were eager to tour the latest addition to St. Peter's. Joe passed it on foot every morning and had yet to even look in through the glass door.

DR. JOE PACHOREK (GERALD MCRANEY) IS CALLED UPON TO OPERATE ON THE DRUNK DRIVER WHO KILLED HIS CHILDREN

The atrium project was Lisa's brainchild. She had raised most of the money herself and had spent countless hours sculpting an original piece for the entry. She must have taken a break from the auction benefit to see that it was delivered safely and installed in just the right spot. Joe watched as she followed the men into the building.

He was startled by a rap on his door.

"Come in," he called without thinking. He didn't want to see or talk to anyone.

That woman, Monica, the one who called herself the transplant liaison, stepped cautiously into the room.

"Dr. Pachorek, I know it's bold of me to barge in here like this, but I've been told of your—your situation. They haven't had much success finding another surgeon. I know you can't imagine going ahead with this, but I'm here to see it through and will do anything I can to help."

Joe turned back toward the window and stared out silently. "Weird world, isn't it?" he said after a moment. "What are the odds of this happening?"

"The laws of probability never seem to matter when something's happening to you," Monica replied.

"I've been a prisoner of probability," Joe sneered.

"Chance disappears when you make a decision," Monica said.

Joe pressed his fingers deeply into the back of the tufted leather chair where he stood.

"Oh, I made my decision a long time ago," he said slowly. "I promised myself that if I ever saw that pathetic creature again, I would kill him with my bare hands."

Callie pulled an article from the envelope Chris handed her. "Drunk driver pleads guilty in death of five," she read aloud.

"Oh, ye of little faith." Monica beamed as she took the newspaper from Callie. There, in the middle of the page, was the scarred face and the sad eyes of the convicted killer staring blankly up at her.

"He killed five kids and all he gets is a scar on his face?" Callie said, grabbing the paper back.

"Uh, Callie . . ." Chris looked as if he wanted to say something, but Ms. Martin waved him off.

"I'll see you back at the office," she told him. "Thanks."

With a disappointed look, he walked away, and Callie turned back to Monica. "Okay, he existed," Callie conceded. "But where's the headline that says this piece of scum died? I mean, how could anyone seriously consider giving this guy a second chance? And please, don't even *think* about telling me this is God's will."

Monica sighed. "I knew this was going to be a tough assignment once I realized Ethan only had seven hours to live."

"How did you know that?" Callie looked at her suspiciously.

"I saw Andrew."

"Andrew?"

"The angel of death."

"There's an angel of death," Callie said in a monotone.

"Let me finish my story."

Monica, knowing there was no more she could do for Joe at the moment, left him with his bitter thoughts and turned her attention to Ethan. She found the weak and frightened man in a section of the emergency room that was curtained off for privacy. Andrew sat vigilantly at the end of Ethan's movable bed.

"Is he going to . . ." Monica whispered.

"I'm here early," Andrew whispered back. "To help Ethan get used to the idea."

"Then he is going to die?" She frowned. Her role in all of this was becoming increasingly confusing.

He shook his head. "I didn't say that, Monica. Right now this man is your assignment, not mine. It's my understanding that you've got until midnight to see that this situation gets resolved."

The time was 4:59 P.M.

Even with his marriage in shambles and the couple barely speaking to each another, there were times when Joe knew that the only person who could possibly understand him was his wife, Lisa. Together, they had survived the years of medical school and art school. And the five beautiful babies that followed. They had shared so many experiences. Now, as he faced this horrible dilemma, he found himself longing for his wife's listening ear and compassionate heart. If only he knew how to talk to her.

It was shortly after six o'clock when he locked up the office, rode the elevator to the ground level, and walked across the entryway toward the newest hospital expansion project. Bright orange construction barriers blocked the entryway, where, propped beside a ladder, was a sign waiting to be installed: "Pachorek Children's Wing." The sight was almost more than Joe could bear. A permanent monument to his children. And all of it courtesy of a man who now expected Dr. Joe Pachorek to extend his miserable life.

Suddenly, he spotted Lisa. By the wide-eyed look on her face, she was obviously as startled as he was. She held the corner of a heavy gray packing quilt that completely blanketed the sculpture. Three workers stood nearby, as if waiting for directions.

Joe wanted to say something, anything to feel the intimacy again that they had known years before. But any meaningful words he might have spoken clogged in his throat.

"Uh, I'm sorry," he murmured. "I didn't mean to interrupt." He turned and hurried back outside.

Monica was sitting beside Ethan's bed when she first heard the voice of Dr. Pachorek's wife, Lisa. She moved aside the curtain drawn around Ethan's bed and saw Lisa coming down the hallway, asking first an orderly, then a nurse, then an intern, if they had seen her husband.

"I know he was supposed to be performing a heart transplant tonight," she said to a desk clerk stationed near Monica and Ethan. "Dr. Joseph Pachorek—do you have his schedule?"

Beside Monica, Ethan stirred. "Oh, dear God," was all he could manage. "Dear God, no."

"The transplant for Mr. Ethan Parker," the nurse replied, looking down at Joe's notes on the chart. "I'm not sure where Dr. Pachorek has gone."

"What? Ethan Parker—" A wild look came into Lisa's eyes.

"I saw the doctor a few minutes ago in the parking lot," an orderly said as he passed by.

Lisa turned then and ran toward the elevators.

Ethan looked up at Monica.

"I'm Monica, the transplant coordinator," she introduced herself and smiled down at him. "We've got a lot of work to do tonight, and you've got a lot to live for, my friend."

She squeezed his hand and then saw a small glimmer of something in his eyes. It was hope; she had seen it many times before.

Joe stood alone, shirt untucked, hair rumpled, head down, and leaning on the hood of his prized German sports car. One glance at Lisa as she crossed the parking lot toward him, and he knew that she knew.

"I heard," was all she said. She paused for a moment, then, "Are you going to say something to me? Just one word? Maybe fill your quota for the year?"

"I've been thinking. When we buried our babies, I stopped believing in God—" Joe started to explain, but Lisa cut him short.

"Remember how Sylvie would look at the stars and ask where God lived and you'd say, 'Right here,' and touch her heart?"

"Stop that, Lisa," he countered. "There is no God. No, maybe there is. I don't know. How could I hate Him so much if He doesn't exist?"

Lisa stared at him. "I think it's me you hate," she said slowly.

"Oh, c'mon, Lisa, that's crazy ..."

"Is it? I don't think so. Why don't you just admit it? I see it every time you look at me. You blame me. I took the kids out. I used my car. Why couldn't I have just waited for the stupid basketball game—"

"All right!" Joe exploded. "You're right! If you'd just waited a few lousy minutes, our kids would still be alive! I told you I'd do it! I told you! Five minutes, that's all. Five minutes—"

"You just sat there!" Lisa screamed back at him. "Why didn't you just take them when I asked you to? Why didn't you listen to your children for once . . ."

"I don't know," he moaned. "I don't know." He turned to his car and gave the side a vicious kick.

"You want to blame me," Lisa said after a moment. She was calmer now. "You want to blame God. You don't care who gets blamed just as long as you don't have to blame yourself."

Joe looked at her. What was she talking about?

"I've forgiven him, Joe," she went on. "And I've forgiven myself, and you, and God, and basketball, and snow, and everything else I blamed. And it's slow, but I'm starting to get my life back. I want it back." She paused. "With or without you."

Joe shook his head. "Can you honestly look me in the eye and tell me you've forgiven that monster?"

"If I don't, I'll die too."

"Oh, really? So you're all over it now? You must be. I mean, you spend every waking minute raising money to finish that children's wing. And the rest of the time you disappear into that studio of yours and stab at your chunks of bronze." Joe saw the look of agony on Lisa's face, but he couldn't seem to stop talking. "You think I don't know what that children's wing is? You know why I can't walk inside that stinking place? It's not a memorial to our children. It's your way of reminding me of the biggest mistake of my entire life. And you made sure I'd have to walk by it every day. Well, I will. But no way will I ever stand inside of it and pretend I'm over this." He sighed and leaned on the car. "The truth is, Lisa, one minute this way or that—what's the difference?" He shook his head. "It didn't matter who took the kids because . . . because he got into his car that day. He's the one." He breathed deeply. "And he should have died in that crash along with them."

Lisa waited. "Don't come home until you've forgiven that man in there," she said finally. "And yourself. And me and God . . ."

Joe watched as his wife walked back toward the hospital.

Monica, hiding in the evening's shadows, dropped her head into her hands. She was consumed with fear for the young man whose life was seeping away and grief-stricken for the Pachoreks who just couldn't seem to hear one another. It all seemed hopeless, and Monica could not seem to move the situation in any kind of positive direction. Every time she turned around, something seemed to be getting worse.

"Dear Father," she prayed. "I am so helpless here. One man has died, another is almost gone, and one is dying inside and doesn't even know it. Please give me the wisdom to know how to help Ethan and how to reach Joe."

It took Joe almost an hour to recover from the bout with Lisa. After pacing back and forth through a park next to the hospital, he stuffed his shirttail back into his pants, wiped his face with a handkerchief, and walked back into the building. He expected to hear that another surgical team was on the way over.

Instead, he came up behind two of the on-duty nurses who were speaking in hushed tones just outside of the room where he knew Ethan Parker waited for a heart transplant.

"We've run out of time—and options," one said to the other. "We've called the only other doctors who could possibly do this transplant. The patient is going down fast. The young climber's heart is healthy, and it's a perfect match."

"The patient found out who would be doing the surgery," the other nurse said. "He acted like he'd almost rather die than face him. Can you imagine? No one will believe it was a mistake if this patient dies. If Dr. Pachorek doesn't do the surgery, he could lose everything."

Joe turned toward the elevator, eager to escape before they saw him. His mind was racing. What should he do? At the ping of the elevator, the doors opened and he quickly stepped inside. Then suddenly, someone on the hospital staff—it looked like Monica—pushed a gurney into the elevator after him. But she didn't get in. She stepped back, and since the gurney blocked the row of buttons, Joe couldn't reach them to push the one that would hold the door open.

"Hey! What—" Joe looked down at the man on the gurney and found himself face-to-face with Ethan Parker. Horror-stricken to be in this enclosed space with his children's killer, he frantically struggled to reach across Parker for the elevator buttons. But he didn't even want to get that close to him. He was suddenly terrified of the tremor in his hands and the evil thoughts racing through his mind.

"I've had this heart thing all my life," Parker murmured, his voice watery and weak. "Nobody thought I'd make it to twelve, then fifteen, then twenty. When I made it to twenty-five, I thought I had it beat. But . . . the day after my birthday, they told me no way, I'd be lucky to make it to dinner, let alone thirty. So I kinda went crazy, started drinking—"

Joe lifted his palms upright to cut Ethan off. He didn't want to hear any excuses from this man. No lame 'I'm a victim, too' speech. No sad story about the events that led to his getting drunk that terrible winter day.

"I—don't—care," he stated coldly.

But Ethan kept talking. "I don't know why I'm still alive," he said. "It should have been me. I live with the guilt every day. But if I get another chance, I swear to you, Doctor, I'll use it. I'll try to make some kind of a difference, somehow." He took a deep breath. "But if something happens on that table tonight, I wouldn't blame you."

Joe looked down at the man, the hideous scar across his face, the modest hospital gown that covered his now gangly frame. He couldn't speak. He simply nodded.

The elevator finally lurched to a stop and the doors opened. Joe practically leaped out of the elevator, flagged a nurse's attention, and barked, "Get this guy up to OR."

The harvest of Andy's organs had been set for 8:00 P.M. Joe knew there was no way out of showing up for the surgery. And so he was waiting outside the operating room for the final go-ahead when Monica handed him a copy of the donor card. On the back of the card he read the words: "Take what you need and carry on. I plan to."

"Do you ever wonder why some people have to die before others can live?" Monica pondered aloud. "Or . . ." She cocked her head. "Why enemies live when innocents die?"

Joe knew her questions didn't really demand that he answer. "All the time," he said.

"But you don't know why then," Monica pressed.

Joe shook his head and wished she'd disappear.

"Maybe that's because we're not supposed to know," she mused.

"There's never a good reason for death," Joe said, kicking himself for continuing this conversation.

"You won't know that for sure until you die," Monica said.

He looked at her curiously. Who was this person?

"I'm just saying, how can you judge something fairly when you don't know what the rules are?" Monica continued. "You can't play God, Joe. Because you aren't God."

Back at the restaurant, Tess was refilling the salt, pepper, and sugar shakers, staying busy and looking none too happy about it. It was growing dark outside, and the restaurant had emptied a long time ago.

"This is ridiculous," Callie ranted. "Ethan Parker should never have gotten a chance at a heart in the first place. Somebody should've stopped it before he ever got on a waiting list."

"You, too, then?" Monica said. "You think he deserved to die?"

"Absolutely. Five painful times over. And he only served two years. It's obscene."

"He did a terrible thing, that's true. But you think there's no chance anything good could come out of this?"

"No way. Bad eggs should be thrown out before they stink everything up. I gotta go to the ladies' room." And she slid out of the booth and headed toward the back of the restaurant.

Monica wondered what had happened in Callie's life to make her so calloused and hard-hearted.

"Speaking of throwing people out . . ." Tess stood at Monica's table with a pot of coffee in one hand and Callie's credit card receipt in the other.

"It's taking longer than I thought it would," Monica said apologetically.

Tess rubbed her right shoulder. "Really. This isn't *War and Peace,* you know. I've been on my feet all day, table twelve sent the fish back twice, and if you think I'm gonna pull the dinner shift, too, you better straighten out your halo. Now, finish the story, and let's get outta here."

The door swung open, and Andrew swept into the room. He tipped his hat at each of his coworkers and headed toward the piano bar, almost colliding with Callie on the way.

"Timing is everything now," Tess whispered to Monica as she turned away from the booth.

"Okay, let's wrap this up," Callie said, sliding back into the booth. "Now, there's no one else to do the surgery. He has to do it. But he doesn't have to do it 'right.'"

Monica gasped. "That's a terrible thing to say. Are you always this vengeful?"

"This is a lonely town, you know?" Callie leaned across the table. "You gotta fight for what's yours. Seats on the subway, the next number in line at the deli. I reported the people next door for lifting my Sunday paper. So if somebody actually took away something I really loved—I'd nail them in a New York minute, and I wouldn't look back."

"That's what you believe in, then? Getting even?"

"No one ever did me any favors. No humans, no angels. Me. That's what I believe in. Don't ask me to believe in anything else." She sat back in the booth. "Unless you got proof."

Monica didn't answer right away. Piano music drifted to them from the back of the restaurant. Andrew was warming up. She felt a sudden sadness overtake her as she studied the attractive woman across from her. Then, in spite of herself, she smiled.

"I'll see what I can do," she said.

It was after 8:00 when Joe and his assembled transplant team began to scrub up in preparation for the intricate surgery. Joe could feel his agitation increasing as he scrubbed and polished his arms and hands. Suddenly everything reminded him of his kids. As he reached for a towel, memories of their nightly baths came flooding forward in his thoughts. The scent of baby shampoo and the feel of their soft clean pajamas. *Goodnight, Moon* and *The Runaway Bunny*. The purple dinosaur on Sylvie's pillowcase . . .

A nurse tied Joe's mask, and he backed into the operating room.

The tension was ominous. In Joe. In his colleagues. In the eyes that peered over the masks of every person in the room, and those who watched from the theater above. After several moments, the door swung open and a nurse carefully carried in Andy's heart in a simple metal bowl. Joe tried not to consciously think about who his patient was as he removed the man's diseased heart and placed it in a receptacle. The nurse presented the new heart to Joe in what appeared an almost sacrificial gesture. He took the bowl, peered inside, and gave his assistant a nod.

"Give me some light in here," Joe demanded, his agitation increasing. When nothing happened immediately, he yelled, "Light, I said!" He looked up from his patient quickly and saw the second hand on the clock stop at 10:06 P.M.

Joe turned his head, feeling suddenly woozy. No one in the room was moving. Sweat beaded on his forehead. Was he about to black out? He looked down. He held the new heart in his hands—the heart that would give his children's killer new life.

"Joe!" the nurse standing across from him called out. Monica removed her mask. It was as if everything stopped as she spoke.

"I told you before. I'm here to see you through this." A bright light filled the area of the operating room where she stood. "I'm an angel, Joe."

Joe squinted, wiped his face on the sleeve of his scrubs, and looked back at her again.

"That is your own life you're holding in your hands. And you can't save it any more than you can save or take Ethan's life. There is only one Physician in the room tonight. He's the One who gave you the talent to save lives, and only He has the right to take a life or to give one back. Let Him give yours back to you, Joe. Let Him help you find mercy for those who fail."

Joe shook his head. "I—I can't. I don't know how . . ."

"That's why I'm here. God loves you. And whether you think He should or not, He loves this man Ethan. He wants this to be a room of life, not death. But He can do nothing unless you get out of the way. Let go of your guilt, and release this man from his. With Andy's heart, Ethan can carry on. And so can you."

"My children," Joe said, the agony of the moment tearing at his insides. "Who will carry on for them?"

"The children are carrying on just fine," Monica said reassuringly.

And with that, the clock began to tick again. Joe let his breath out, the breath of a spirit in the process of renewal.

"You okay, Joe?" someone asked.

Joe looked around him as if seeing his staff for the first time. Then he looked down at the man on the table before him. He nodded. "Let's do it." With steady hands, he lifted Andy's heart from the bowl and skillfully placed it into Ethan's chest.

The rest of the procedure continued with textbook precision. When the final sutures were in place and each monitor was sending the correct signal, Joe gave a nurse the go-ahead to release blood from a bypass into a tube recycling into Ethan. Then doctors, nurses, and attendants all waited anxiously to gauge the patient's response.

"Heart's going to take any second now." Joe glanced from tube to monitor and back again. "Any second, let's go now."

But then Ethan's new heart began fibrillating.

"Paddles!" Joe yelled.

"Paddles," a nurse responded and handed them to Joe. After applying the paddles, Joe stepped back.

"Clear, charge to twenty . . . shock," called a voice.

Nothing.

"Again," Joe cried, now perspiring heavily through his mask and cap. "He's still fibrillating. Check the electrolytes. Venous blood gas, okay?"

The profusionist nodded frantically. Joe feared the worst, that air had entered Ethan's coronary arteries and the heart would be rejected. He was certain everything had gone right—blood should now be pumping through Ethan's chest.

"Doctor, the clamps have been off for two minutes," a nurse warned.

Joe yanked off his mask, inhaled deeply, lifted the sheet that covered Ethan Parker, and took the man's lifeless hand in his own. He squeezed it gently and lowered his head to Ethan's ear. "Carry on," he whispered.

A moment later Ethan's heart finally began to pump. Everyone in the operating room gave a collective sigh and then a loud hurrah. Monica, back in her scrub suit, wore a smile as wide as her face.

Joe peeled off his gloves, mask, hat, and gown, and walked out of the operating room. With determined strides, he continued down the main hallway that led to the new hospital wing. At the doorway, he paused for several moments. Under a spotlight, in the middle of the room, stood Lisa's unblanketed work of art. The life-sized bronze statue was an actual park-like setting with a tree, fountain, and five laughing children piled together on a sled.

Joe reached down to touch the cool cheek of his youngest daughter, then straightened when he saw movement out of the corner of his eye.

Lisa stood in the doorway watching him.

"It's so beautiful," he murmured, then held his arms out to his wife. She didn't hesitate but practically ran into his arms. And for the first time since their children's deaths, they wept together. Without accusations. Without bitterness. Without blame.

Callie seemed moved by Monica's sensitive recounting of the way the lives of Andy, Joe, and Ethan had intertwined. But it was hard to tell. The woman was a master of stoicism.

"So, this drunk driver," she said, clearing her throat. "He survived? I don't get it."

"It wasn't his time," Monica said.

"What a waste of a good heart." Callie slapped a few dollars on the table, snatched up her blazer, and stood to her feet. "You told me that when you'd finished your story, I'd believe in angels. Well, I think you're nuts, at the very least. I said I needed proof in order to do a story. That's what I still need."

Callie brushed some crumbs from the front of her skirt and headed toward the door. The three angels were suddenly left alone in the candlelit restaurant. Andrew stopped playing the piano, but Tess simply removed her apron and flashed Monica her trademark smile.

Monica watched from the doorway as Callie stood on the curb buttoning her rumpled jacket. Then she ripped the tape from her recorder and slam-dunked it into a nearby trash bin.

Callie dropped the recorder back in her purse and glanced up at the traffic signal across the street. By that time, Monica had joined Andrew at the base of the signal pole. Callie seemed startled to see them as she stepped off the curb.

Suddenly, out of nowhere, a bus bore down on her. With lightning speed, a bystander tackled Callie to get her out of the way, and they rolled across the street and out of the vehichle's path. He had just saved her life.

Obviously shaken, Callie let her rescuer help her to her feet in front of where Monica and Andrew had stood only a moment before. Monica watched as the realization dawned on Callie's face when she saw the unmistakable scar that that identified her rescuer. It was Ethan Parker.

"You okay?" he asked.

"I—I think so," Callie choked out. "Thanks."

"I'm just glad I was here to help." And he disappeared into the throng of rush-hour pedestrians.

Monica tapped Callie on the shoulder. "Now I'm finished with my story," she said with a smile.

THREE HAPPY ANGELS WAVE GOOD-BYE TO CALLIE
(DELLA, ROMA & BRUCE ALTMAN)

Callie's eyes widened and she dashed around the front end of an idling taxi. Then she hurried back across the street to the trash bin to find the cassette tape she'd just thrown away. It was the proof she'd been looking for. But before she could make it to the curb, a garbage truck pulled up, and in one fell swoop, scooped up the trash bin with a powerful arm and emptied the contents over the top.

The truck set the trash bin back down, then rolled on past her. Three uniformed trash handlers clung to the back of the truck with one hand and waved to her with the other. When Callie recognized Monica, Tess, and Andrew, they gave the reporter a collective grin the size of Central Park.

Then Monica tossed the cassette tape into the air, where it became a white dove and flew off toward the heavens. ⌒

Response to the Show

Roma Downey

I have a very good friend who is a priest back in Ireland. *Touched by an Angel* has just started airing there and is in the top twenty. He uses this particular show, "Interview with an Angel," as a teaching tool with the children of his parish. He pauses the video right before the doctor makes his decision and asks the students what the doctor should do and why. I love the idea that the show could be used in that way. As an actor I particularly loved that episode because I had the chance to play some comedy in the early scenes.

Gerald McRaney—Dr. Joe Pachorek

This was an episode that really touched a nerve, especially for parents, many of whom were disturbed by the idea of losing a child and then coming face-to-face with the killer. It was a deeply emotional role to play, but the sensitive subject matter was presented so believably, and the outcome was very uplifting. I'm not sure there is another show that would have dealt with something like this, let alone nearly as well. When CBS came calling with the pilot for *Promised Land*, I was eager to work again with the talented and inspired production team that brings America *Touched by an Angel*.

Marcia Strassman—Lisa Pachorek

I'm a parent, and a parent's worst nightmare is that something bad will happen to her child. Lisa was ready to forgive this man, but I wasn't sure that as a parent I ever could. The thought of giving birth to five children and having them wiped out in an instant—I don't know what kind of inner strength it would take to forgive their killer.

But in the story God's plan was that this man should live. There was a reason for him to be on the planet. It was a battle of wills between God and mortals.

I love the show. It's nice not to have to wonder what you or your children are watching. I don't want to be assaulted at night in my own home. The morals are great, and it's nice to see a positive spin put on God that isn't sappy.

FROM VIEWERS

I have been suffering from severe depression for over two years. No drugs (or other treatments) have helped. Gradually I had begun to accept the consequences of my choice to end my life. That all changed after I watched *Touched by an Angel* last Saturday night. During the episode the young man was donating his organs, but the doctor's family was killed by the recipient, so the surgeon didn't want to do the procedure. Initially I broke down when I heard the words "Take what you need and carry on." It reaffirmed, I thought, my determination to end my life in a manner that would allow for the transplant of my organs to others in need. The most powerful words came to me when Monica was talking to the doctor and said something like, "You don't have the right to play God. Only God can decide when it's time for someone to die." Those words cut right to my soul. I felt as if Monica was really talking to me. It drastically changed my perspective, and after several sessions with my therapist and psychiatrist, I can honestly say that for the first time in nearly three years I have no thought or feelings of committing suicide.

I know I have a long way to go through therapy, but for some weird reason I haven't been able to accept or understand, I feel like I was "touched by an angel." This is strange because I have been an atheist for more than twenty years, yet I believe a guardian angel must have been looking down on me that night. Thank you again for this miracle.

A viewer from Wisconsin

CHAPTER 3

THERE, BUT FOR THE GRACE OF GOD

Tess: "You took the easy way out. The same
easy way out everybody else takes: you found
yourself an excuse not to get involved."

The Story Behind the Story

It was late autumn in Salt Lake City. *Touched by an Angel* had been on the air only a few months, and it was just barely holding on. The only people I was certain were watching the show were whoever was sitting in my mother's living room.

Gregory Harrison was watching, however. TV's *Trapper John* had become a movie-of-the-week favorite, and a guest star appearance by Gregory guaranteed high ratings. As the head of his own successful production company, he also took note of television trends. And he was the first star to approach us and express interest in appearing on *Touched by an Angel*.

Ever-disciplined, Gregory was the only person getting a workout on the cold basketball court behind the Salt Lake Holiday Inn, where our makeshift offices were that initial season. The rest of us were in parkas and Gregory, on a break from shooting a Utah-based movie, was shooting hoops in T-shirts and shorts. We had worked together on his ABC sitcom *The Family Man* several years earlier. Somehow he recognized me through all the goose down and came bounding across the court with a big grin and a big hug for an old friend.

"I want to be on your show." I was thunderstruck. I was stunned that he had even *seen* the show.

"I want to do something that I will be proud to show my children. Something that matters."

I asked him, "What do you care about?"

Without hesitation he said, "The homeless." And "There, But for the Grace of God" was born. Over several weeks, Gregory and I spoke on the phone, exploring our own concerns and misconceptions about homelessness. The turning point in the story process came the day that Gregory, in frustration, finally blurted out: "Every time I saw a homeless person on the street, subconsciously I assumed they had done something wrong to get there. That there had been a choice involved. That made it easier to look the other way. And I'm ashamed of that."

We decided to write a show that explored lots of reasons why people end up living on the street. And we wanted to remind ourselves of the humanity of people who, but for the grace of God, could be us.

To do that, we wanted to follow a day in the life of several street people, people of different ages, races, gender. We found a golden ensemble of actors in Gregory, Marion Ross

(*Happy Days*, *Brooklyn Bridge*), and Malcolm-Jamal Warner (*The Cosby Show*).

Normally, a script is written and then the casting directors take the script and begin searching for actors to play the roles.

Touched, however, has often taken a different strategy, and it began with this episode. The prestigious casting firm of Reuben Cannon and Associates was a marvelous asset to our show, and from the beginning, Reuben and his talented associate David Giella committed not only their time but their hearts to finding the perfect star for every episode. Sometimes, before the script was ever written.

The second or third question people always ask about *Touched* is: "How do you get such great guest stars?" The answer lies in the passionate belief these two gentlemen have in the power of television to make a positive difference. That was the offer they made to every actor they approached. Their taste was unerring, and often they inspired our scripts rather than the other way around. Through their efforts, the quality was raised from just the "stunt casting" of celebrities to the showcasing of extraordinary talent such as Natalie Cole, Maya Angelou, B. B. King, Olympia Dukakis, Phylicia Rashad, Hal Linden, Stacy Keach, Valerie Harper, Elliot Gould, Brooke Adams, Brian Keith, Gerald McRaney, Joe Morton, Ossie Davis, John Ritter, and others whose names appear in the Appendix.

As a successful film producer, Reuben continues to support quality screen projects (Spike Lee's *Get on the Bus*). David Giella leads the casting of *Touched* as well as *Promised Land*. And whenever possible, we implement the strategy we began on the "homeless episode" of casting before we write.

It was Roma Downey herself who provided the last piece of the puzzle to "There, But for the Grace of God." I told her the story in her trailer on the set. Roma suggested that the angel Monica should become homeless herself in order to truly "share their pain." It was not only a turning point in the development of the script, but of the entire series.

Putting Monica on the "inside" of the problem has been a tremendously successful device. Through her eyes, we discover our own preconceptions about life here on earth. And, once "clipped of her wings," Monica explores the human condition for us as well. Nowhere has her "grounded angel" plight been more powerful than in this episode. It is in the moment of healing, when the homeless and seemingly helpless Monica can perform only one act of love—nothing supernatural, but utterly human and humble: she washes the tortured feet of the hopeless Pete and asks for his forgiveness. In that transforming moment, they are both healed.

I have seen grown men in Armani suits shed tears when that single scene has been shown in meetings. After it aired, I heard from an emergency room nurse who has since made it a practice to wash the feet of every destitute patient who enters her hospital. Later, I discovered that Gregory Harrison donated his entire acting fee to Habitat for Humanity, the organization supported by former President Jimmy Carter that builds homes *with* the homeless *for* the homeless. There stands in Los Angeles today a house—a home—that was not there before. It shelters a family because one man stopped what he was doing to get involved and give what he could "to do something that matters."

—M. W.

THERE, BUT FOR THE GRACE OF GOD

TELEPLAY BY MARTHA WILLIAMSON
AND R. J. COLLEARY
STORY BY MARTHA WILLIAMSON

"Just remember this, angel baby," admonished
Tess. "Pride goeth before a fall." Okay, Monica had
heard the quotation; she'd even used it. But, for
example, why shouldn't she be proud of her latest
success: seeing a young couple reunited? Hadn't it
been some of her best work? She was still a novice,
and her mentor could see that Monica had momen-
tarily lost sight of who deserved the real credit.
Hence Monica's next assignment . . .

*P*ete's recurring nightmare jolted him from a deep
sleep yet once again. He rubbed his eyes, then
slowly sat up and looked around the quiet alley.

In his dream, Pete had held a cardboard sign reading:
"Help. Need work." He had positioned himself near a free-
way on-ramp early one weekday morning and hoped a compassionate soul would stop. Eventually, a man in a new
midnight blue van, also Pete, pulled over, asked what kind of
work the homeless Pete could do, and offered him $7.50 an
hour to lay carpet.

"I'm sorry, but I don't think I can do that," the homeless Pete told the middle-class Pete. "My knees are shot."

The driver of the van was incensed by the man's response. He had gone out of his way to help the scraggly, unshaven "street person" who, from all appearances, was clearly on the down and out.

"You ever stop to think maybe it's that attitude that got you here in the first place?" the driver shouted. He rolled up the window in disgust and sped on up the ramp.

The man he once was came face-to-face with the person he had become.

Now, ten feet away from him, the same Chevy van sat on bald tires, its paint weathered and license sticker expired. Pete stood to his feet, picked up a filthy red gym bag that doubled as a pillow, and walked back to his vehicle. Better to stay close to his wheels in case someone came by to prod him along.

Monica and Tess perched on a fire escape across the alley and watched as Pete moved furtively from the doorway of the cafe into his van.

"I'll never understand how people can let themselves go like that." Monica shook her head in amazement.

"You will soon," Tess said with a wry smile. "He's your next assignment."

"He is?" Monica said in a less than enthusiastic tone. She saw a stretch of time before her with a dearth of festive holiday gatherings, restored relationships, newborn babies, or interesting food. She yawned slightly. "So what is it—volunteering in a shelter or counseling the homeless?"

"None of the above," Tess said.

"Well, then, how can I—"

"Monica, the only way to share this man's pain is to share his pain."

"Oh no." She was starting to get it, but she didn't like it.

"Here, let me help you with that." Tess turned Monica around by the shoulders and helped the startled angel peel off her beautiful wool winter coat. Next came the coordinating beret. Monica could keep the knit scarf.

Then, in a second, she was transformed, and given an entirely new look, one she'd never seen in any of the fashion magazines she'd observed humans reading. Her new coat was baggy and threadbare and hung almost to her ankles. Under the coat she wore a pair of frayed blue jeans, shiny with wear, an acrylic pullover, and an oversized man's plaid shirt. She looked down to see her fingers wrapped in cotton rags and her feet shod in a pair of lightweight socks and laceless yellow sneakers.

A film of dirt covered her new attire. When she looked up, she saw that Tess was gone.

Suddenly conscious of her freezing hands and feet, she eyed a dumpster directly behind the cafe where she'd seen the homeless man earlier. Perhaps she could find something in the trash that might help keep her warm. She was eager to put on an extra layer of anything at all. She reached into the trash and in a moment, pulled out a worn black glove. Encouraged, she reached back in, but this time her fingers touched something cold and slimy.

"Yech!" she exclaimed and pulled her hand out quickly. "This is disgusting." She was already tired of her new role. Where was Tess?

"The nerve of people," a scratchy voice behind her spoke, causing her to jump. "Throwing out garbage."

MONICA FINDS HERSELF HOMELESS IN
"THERE, BUT FOR THE GRACE OF GOD"

"You frightened me," she told the scraggly man carrying the bulky zippered bag. It had been patched many times over with tape.

"What are you doing here?" the man asked in an accusing tone, as if she'd invaded his private domain.

"I was just looking for something to help me keep warm."

"Aren't we all?" He glared at her. "This is *my* alley."

"Your alley?"

"My alley," he repeated, then motioned around him. "This is *my* van, this is *my* dumpster, and this is *my* alley."

"Please," she said in her kindest Irish voice. "I found this one glove. I was hoping there might be another one in here somewhere."

"Well, let's see what we have here," he said more warmly as he bent over to rifle through the dumpster's contents himself. "Pardon the mess," his muffled voice rose up to her, "maid's day off. Okay, here's a lighter. Hold it for me." A small silver lighter came flying out of the dumpster. "A comb . . ." She caught the blue comb in midair.

"I don't think so," she said, turning it over in her hands. She threw it back in.

"I don't know what this is or was," he mumbled, "and aha—a glove."

She caught the glove and then pulled both gloves over her hands. A little thrill rose up inside of her. It must not take much to make a homeless person happy.

"Hey, all right!" he yelled, holding up a pair of shoes, covered with something like spackle or paint, dusty and creased with wear. "Today's my lucky day." He paused. "In a manner of speaking." He held out his hand. "The name's Pete."

"Monica," she said, taking his hand.

Pete sat down next to the dumpster and removed the old rags that covered his feet. His bare feet were blistered, cracked, and bleeding with sores. Monica cringed. He then brushed off his "new" shoes and tried to squeeze his feet into them. They were obviously much smaller than a man of Pete's height and build would wear.

"I use a lot of words out here," he said. "Picky is not one of them."

Pete walked slowly, and it seemed almost painfully, down the alley to get used to the feel of the shoes. Monica followed him to the corner and turned when he did. She would have to tag along and look for any clue as to her role in the transformation of his life.

"Haven't seen you around here before," Pete said as they moved down the block.

"I'm not from around here," she told him.

"Me neither."

"Where are you from?" she asked, hoping she wasn't prying beyond what he wanted to share.

"Someplace else," he said vaguely. "Well, this is where I need to leave you. There's a Mission on Flower Street two blocks up. You can't sleep there except in bad weather, but they'll feed you."

So this assignment *would* come with some food. Monica was relieved to hear it, and was ready to sit down to a plate of anything hot, and especially a cup of coffee.

"Thank you, I'll see you there," she said.

"Oh, no, you won't." He shook his head. "I'm not homeless. I'm just saving my pennies to get my van fixed so I can go to Colorado."

Monica looked him up and down before she could stop herself. "I'm sorry. I thought . . ."

"Well, the clothing budget isn't what it used to be . . ." He looked down at his threadbare shirt, dirty trousers, and holey jacket. "I'm saving anything I can earn for the van. Look, I've gotta go. I've got to get to work." He turned to head up the sidewalk.

"Wait," she called after him. "Your lighter."

But he just waved her off. "Keep it. Maybe you can trade it for something you need. It's the way of the street."

She watched as he walked away, a man with nothing in his pockets and the burden of the world on his shoulders. But then maybe it wasn't so bad. He wasn't homeless, after all. And he had a car, a job, and a goal. She turned around to go back toward the alley and walked right into Tess.

"Your assignment just walked away," Monica's supervisor scolded, right eyebrow aloft.

"Oh, he'll be fine." Monica eyed Tess's fur-lined jacket and wool pants. She had been homeless long enough to feel the pain now. She hoped Tess would agree with her. She would certainly be more understanding of homeless people in the future. "He's got a job," she went on lightly, "a head on his shoulders, a plan to move on . . . I think he's going to make it."

"You think so, huh?" Tess looked at her closely. "Is that Monica the angel saying that or Monica the cold and hungry and give-me-back-my-coat who's saying that?"

Monica was confused. As she saw it, she had met Pete, her assignment, and helped him find shoes. They had talked. Then he had gone to work. The man didn't need an angel anymore. This case was closed.

"Have I done something wrong?" she asked innocently.

"You took the easy way out." Tess stood with her hands on her hips and looked sternly at Monica. "It's the same easy way out everybody else takes. You found yourself an excuse not to get involved."

"But he doesn't need me—"

"Wrong! He doesn't *want* to need you or anybody else. His self-esteem may be shot, but he's still got his pride."

Just then a woman around sixty years of age pushed a shopping cart past Tess and Monica on the sidewalk. She was jabbering incoherently to herself. File folders, spiral notebooks, and crumpled paper spilled out of the cart, but the woman didn't seem to notice. Monica watched her amble down the street, then turned back to Tess.

"So tell me what I'm supposed to do!" This assignment—helping a person who is already helping himself—made little sense.

"Don't you raise your voice to me, Miss Wings," Tess said indignantly. "You got a little pride thing goin' on yourself."

Monica's shoulders sagged. What was wrong with her? "I'm sorry, I don't know what's come over me. I'm cold. I itch. I think I even feel hungry. I don't feel like myself. In fact, I don't even feel like an angel anymore."

"Your assignment is not to feel like an angel. It's to feel something else altogether. This man Pete, he's a fighter. But he's been hit too many times. One blow after the other. Too hard and too fast. And the next blow could put him down and keep him down. And pride is not gonna help that. Not his. And not yours. You better hang on to that lighter. You're going to need it."

And once again, Tess was gone, leaving Monica alone on the street.

"The lighter. What have I done with the lighter?" Monica started fishing through her pockets to find it again. Not in the left breast pocket. Not in her jeans. She began to panic, searching frantically through every fold of her clothing until finally she felt it through a hole in her shirt pocket. It was lodged down in the lining. She pulled it out. "Ah, there you are." She held it tightly in the palm of her right hand. "Hey, lady, look out!" Monica looked up to see a young man on a bicycle headed straight for her. He swerved to avoid hitting her, and she jumped back against a nearby building. The lighter flew from her hand, skittered across the street, and plunged down through a grate in the gutter.

"Oh, no!" she cried.

The hazards of street life. She crossed the street and approached the gutter where she'd seen the lighter disappear.

She crouched down, leaned over the gutter, and

extended her hand as far as it would reach. This was worse than reaching into the dumpster. She would definitely not remember this episode as one of her favorite angel experiences. She moved her hand around. Nothing.

She bent down closer to peer into the gutter.

"I'll get it." A man's voice rose up to her from beneath the street.

Surprised, she backed away. "Thank you, thank you," she said. "It's very important." She had no idea why, but if Tess said to hang onto it, it must be important.

"Yeah, if it's so important, give me a dollar for it," said the opportunist.

"A dollar?" The nerve of some of these street people. "I don't have a dollar. I don't have anything."

"You got gloves," came the quick reply.

"Oh no. Not my gloves."

"No gloves, no lighter."

"There's one lighter, you get one glove," she countered. She couldn't believe she was having this conversation.

"Which hand?" he asked.

"Your choice."

"Right hand."

"Deal."

A hand passed her lighter up through the bars. On the third finger Monica saw a ring engraved with the insignia of the United States Marine Corps.

"Thank you," she said, as she dropped the right-hand glove down through the grate.

"Pleasure doing business with you," the voice said out of the darkness. "Drink?" he asked, extending a vile-smelling paper bag up through the opening.

"No, but thank you." It was always the thought that counted. "Wait, this is silly," she said. "You need both gloves down there. Take the other one, too."

"Nah, keep it," he said. "A deal's a deal."

Monica tucked the lighter into a more secure pocket, then stood to her feet and headed back toward Pete's alley. She was eager to find him and get busy in her role of helping him get out of his sad predicament. If things went well, she could be back before dark in Tess's Cadillac with the heat turned high.

Pete wasn't in the alley, but from the entry, she could see him in the middle of a nearby intersection. His worn-out bag was flung over one shoulder, and he was using both hands to wash the windshields of unhappy motorists who were caught at the red light.

"So that's his job," Monica mumbled as she watched him spray and wipe on one side, then hobble around in pain to the other.

"You're a little young to be talking to yourself," said a woman's voice nearby.

Monica turned to see the lady with the overflowing shopping cart.

"Hello—my name is Monica," she introduced herself to the bag lady.

"I'm Sophie," the woman answered. "You ever been to Dallas?"

"Texas? No, never."

"A likely story." The woman frowned and shook her head. "Well, somebody assassinated him, but nobody's ever been to Dallas. People lie."

"What are all those books?" Monica asked, trying to hide her amusement.

SOPHIE (MARION ROSS) AND MONICA

"Research and evidence. Theories and responses to theories. Diagrams and random notes. Witnesses and suspects."

"Are we talking about the Kennedy assassination?" Monica asked, proud of her knowledge of American history. Angels didn't have to keep up on it.

But Sophie looked suspicious. "What do you know about it all of a sudden?"

"I've just heard of it," Monica said quickly. It wouldn't do to make Sophie think she might be guilty of assassinating the president, at least not before she'd had time to establish some kind of a rapport with the strange woman.

But Sophie didn't seem worried about it anymore. "Do you know what the temperature is?" she asked.

"No, I don't . . ."

"Forty-three degrees." She held up a thermometer. "If you don't know how cold it is, you don't know how cold to be."

Pete methodically pushed the broom back and forth across the cement floor of the cafe. Every evening, when rush hour was over and he was finished cleaning car windows at the intersection, the owner of the cafe gave him a few bucks to stack chairs and sweep out the joint. This was in addition to letting him park his van in the parking lot. Then, when the guy's wife had gone on upstairs to bed, he would sneak some food into a box for Pete to take back to his van.

He leaned his broom up against the back door now, tucked his box under his arm, and climbed up into the back of his van. Squatting on the matted blue shag carpeting, he opened the box to find a cheeseburger, a few french fries, a packet of catsup, and a piece of lemon meringue pie. He grabbed a piece of white china from his small pile of plates in the corner of the van.

A few years ago Pete and his wife once sat down to meals together and used these same plates. He remembered the many nights he would stab at his food but be interrupted by Julie before he could get a bite to his mouth.

"Hey, hey!" she would stop him. "We don't eat in this house until we give thanks."

"Right, sorry," he would mumble, then smile sheepishly at her and clasp his hands. "For all we eat and all we wear," he would pray then, "for daily bread and loving care, we thank Thee, Lord. Amen."

He would start to bring the food to his mouth again, and once again she would stop him. "Wait! We also don't eat in this house until the cook gets a kiss."

He sighed. How he missed her lovely face across from him at dinner. And all day long.

Pete jumped when he heard a knock on the van window. He parted the curtains and cautiously peered out into the alley, then frowned. It was the little street waif he'd met earlier. He hoped she didn't think she could come by for a free meal. He only had enough for himself. With a look of longing at the cheeseburger, he pushed the back door open and stepped out into the darkness.

"What are you doing here?" he barked.

"I didn't know where else to go—"

"Well, find somewhere," he said. "I don't want you hanging around here. If you're gonna live on the streets, you have to learn to live on the streets. You can't count on anybody out here, not even me. I'm going to Colorado anyway, so you can just move along."

"I thought homeless people helped each other out," Monica said, confused.

"I'm *not* homeless!" he yelled impatiently. "I told you. I'm not a bum."

From the look on her face, he was pretty sure he'd gotten the message across. He turned and climbed back into his van, shutting the door hard behind him. She would have to find somewhere else to go. You had to learn to fend for yourself if you lived on the streets. He'd had to. He bit into his cheeseburger.

Monica walked on through the silent city, past the countless people who slept in cartons and tents, warmed themselves by campfires, and huddled together under blankets and newspapers. Some were fortunate enough to have cars. She was shocked to see an entire family of seven sitting upright and trying to sleep in a small sedan.

Monica climbed over a small railing and dropped to her feet under an overpass, out of the biting night wind. She wasn't alone, far from it, but no one around her spoke or even acknowledged her presence. Was there some unwritten code of silence among those who lived without walls?

She pulled her knees up to her chest and bowed her head into her hands. "Don't do this to me, Tess," she cried. "I beg you. In the name of God, please."

When she received no response, she leaned back against a cement wall and tried to sleep.

The next morning, she rose to a stiff neck and sore muscles when the sun penetrated the tunnel. Those who had shared the space the night before were already gone, probably off to find a meal, a shower, a job that would pay enough to exist another day. Some would take their places at a street corner or strip mall, while others would walk their youngsters to school. Most would just hang out, trying to avoid trouble and the police.

Monica stood up slowly, rotating her neck first to the left, and then to the right. As she walked out from beneath the highway, she squinted into the warm sun. She had survived the night, which she hoped would make some kind of an impression on Tess. In spite of how he'd treated her the night before, she needed to find Pete now and complete the task she was sent here for, whatever that was.

In the alley, Monica found the van locked up and its owner nowhere in sight. She walked toward the mission district where she found him sitting alone on a bench at a bus stop. She watched as he reached into a trash container to retrieve a wadded up newspaper. He opened it and began to read.

"Do this every morning?" she asked hesitantly, expecting him to start yelling again when he saw her.

"Doesn't everybody start the day with the paper and a cup of coffee?" he said as he lowered the paper and took a sip from his styrofoam cup.

"I came to say something and then I'll leave," Monica promised.

"You could skip the say something and go right to the leaving part," he said, looking straight at her.

"I didn't mean to suggest that you were a bum." There. That should get them back on track. She hoped.

"I don't know how you could ever think that."

Just then a passerby stopped to drop a dollar bill onto his lap. He looked immediately at Monica, obviously embarrassed, then got to his feet and walked down the sidewalk.

"Pete, wait," she called.

But he kept walking. This was not going to be an easy assignment at all.

"Is that his name, Pete?" asked a strangely familiar voice. She turned to see a young African American, no more than twenty-three years old, sitting on the sidewalk with his back against the window of a seedy convenience store. He wore heavy, round-toed black boots, faded military fatigues, and a dark green jacket.

"Yes, do you know him?" she asked.

"See him every day, never knew his name," the young man said. "Never knew he had a name. Lots of folks out here don't."

"I have a name," she said, extending her left hand. "It's Monica."

"Hi, Monica," he said reaching his hand up to her. "I'm Zack."

"Have we met—" She stopped midsentence as she shook his hand. Their gloves matched.

Zack smiled. "The lighter lady."

She smiled back. "It's good to see you again," she said politely, "but if you'll excuse me, I need to catch up with Pete."

"The man may have lost his self-esteem, but he still has his pride. Leave him alone."

She looked at him, puzzled, but then a screech of tires made her turn toward the street. Sophie stood a few feet away in the middle of the crosswalk. Her cart lay on its side, the contents spilled out in every direction. Monica and Zack rushed to help her while the angry driver rolled down his window to deliver a lewd remark and a rude gesture.

Zack stood boldly in front of the car. "Now," he said. "You wanna honk at me?"

The driver backed down, and Zack ran back to help Monica as she set the shopping cart back on its wheels and gathered up the strewn papers and books. Sophie was growing increasingly frustrated as the wind blew her sacred papers in every direction.

When the three of them had finally managed to get everything back into the cart, they made their way to the sidewalk.

"Thank you so much," Sophie said, then looked closely at Monica. "Aren't you that one who talks to herself?" She turned to Zack. "You ever been to Dallas?"

"Yeah."

Her eyes grew wide. "You have?" she asked. "Come on, let me take you kids to lunch."

Sophie knew her way around the Haven of Rest Mission like a suburban housewife at the neighborhood supermarket.

After waiting in line for meat loaf, mashed potatoes and gravy, green beans, and day-old bread, Monica and Zack followed Sophie into the massive dining room where they sat down at an empty corner of a long table. A number of people were scattered around the room, the majority eating alone, and there was a library-like hush throughout.

"I recognize everyone in here," Sophie told them. "They're regulars. We're like a big happy family."

"A big family where no one speaks to each other," Monica said.

"Sounds like my family," Zack added.

"And do you sleep here too?" Monica asked.

"Can't," Sophie said, shoveling a bite of meat loaf into her mouth. Her teeth were yellow and chipped, Monica couldn't help noticing. "No overnights unless it's under forty degrees. Then Tom—he's the manager—nice boy—Tom gets me a special cot downstairs for obvious reasons."

Monica exchanged a glance with Zack.

"Which obvious reasons are those?" Monica asked.

Sophie looked at Monica like she had lost a marble or two, as though she should certainly know the reasons. "Why, the beds are upstairs, of course. I can't sleep upstairs."

MALCOLM-JAMAL WARNER AS ZACK

"Why?" Zack pressed.

She gave him the same look she'd given Monica. "Why?" she repeated. "Why? Do you know how many people connected to the Kennedy assassination ended up being thrown out of windows?"

"No," Zack said.

Sophie glanced around her and lowered her voice. "Let's just say the amount is disproportionate to the population as a whole."

The gold ring on Zack's left hand caught Monica's eye. "Is that a Marines ring you're wearing?" she asked, glad for an opportunity to change the subject.

"Yeah. I was in the service. Desert Storm."

"Well, you're lucky," Sophie said, patting his hand. "You made it back."

Monica had finished eating and was growing nervous about finding Pete. "I should be going now," she said. "I need to find Pete."

"Is he the one you were checking out yesterday while you were talking to yourself?" Sophie asked.

"Well, yes," Monica said, a little embarrassed.

Sophie nodded. "I see him around. What's he got in that bag he's always carrying?"

"I don't know," Monica said. "But it must be important."

"'Course it is." Zack looked serious for a moment. "In the homeless business, you only carry what keeps you alive."

Pete had made a few dollars washing windows that morning and was headed slowly back to home base. He didn't look forward to now having to sweep out the cafe, but he did look forward to curling up in his van later for a good night's sleep.

He was grateful for his van. So many had to sleep right out in the elements.

But when he turned down the alley, his van was nowhere in sight. He looked around wildly. Where was it? He immediately ran up to the back door of the cafe and pounded with his fists until finally the proprietor's wife opened it a crack.

"My van, my van!" he yelled, near tears.

She looked past him. "It's gone, all right," she said almost gleefully. "Probably junked. Probably flat as a pancake by now. Thank God."

"Where's your husband?" Pete demanded.

"Went to visit his sister for the weekend," she said, nose tilted high. "Now what I say goes. And I say what goes is that van."

"No, no . . ."

"And there's no more dinners, either," she added. "You want to eat? Then get a job, you bum!" She slammed the door in his face.

Pete turned away from the door and stared numbly at the empty space where, until a few hours ago, his van—his home—his way out of the street life—stood. It was always there to offer shelter and warmth. Comforting because he had nothing else. Nothing else at all.

Pete slumped to the ground a few feet away from the back door of the cafe. He lay there, numb with cold and shock, until he fell asleep. He dreamed that night, as he often did, of his beautiful wife. They were lying side by side in bed.

"Can't sleep?" she asked softly.

"No."

"It'll be okay."

"Yeah," he said. But he didn't believe it for a minute.

"Just do what I do," she said, her face aglow. "Keep thinking about Colorado. When this is all over, I'll take you to the top of Mount Thoradin. It's a hard climb, but when you get to the top you just stand there and look out at all these beautiful mountains that are before you, they'll be there after you, and all of a sudden nothing else matters. Just being there, that's what matters."

Pete smiled into the darkness. "They told me not to marry a romantic."

"Promise me, Pete. Promise me we'll go to Colorado."

"I promise."

Sophie and Zack had decided to go along with Monica as she went in search of Pete, and they were all surprised to find him moments later lying in the alley in an almost catatonic state.

"What's he doing lying out here like this?" Monica said, looking around. "Where's his van?"

Pete stared up at them through eyes that were unfocused and full of grief. "My van," he said. "My van . . . is gone."

Monica cupped a hand to her mouth. "Oh, dear God, that's horrible. Dear God, no."

"God can't hear you out here," Zack said.

Monica frowned at him. "God can always hear you," she said.

"Well, maybe He's just ignoring us, then." Zack took a bag in the shape of a bottle from inside his jacket and took a long drink.

"We need to take him somewhere," Sophie said.

"I know a place." Zack reached down to give Pete a hand and then helped him to his feet. Together, they led him across two main boulevards and down through a subterranean gate below the train station. They moved through the large area now populated with many of the city's homeless, including a number of children, and found a deserted corner where they sat down on the cold pavement.

Monica looked around. The walls of the grand terminal were covered with larger-than-life murals depicting an industrious people who had founded the city decades ago. The edifice had now become a sanctuary for the tired, the poor, and the hungry who, for whatever reason, were unable to function outside.

"Excuse me," Sophie addressed a gruff-looking man as he walked by. "Have you ever been to Dallas?"

The man stared at her.

"Hey, it's cool," Zack said to the man, who then walked on. He turned to Sophie. "Please, Sophie, not down here, okay? I have to live with these people."

"You live here?" Monica asked.

Zack nodded. "It's warm and dry. People give each other room, as you can see."

Monica watched as Pete tried to remove his shoes. He winced at the pain, and she couldn't stand it.

"Pete, do you need some help?" she asked.

"No," he said quickly. "Leave me alone."

"Man, why don't you lighten up a little bit?" Zack said.

"Man, why don't you mind your own business?" Pete shot back.

"Zack, how did you find this place?" Sophie asked.

"A couple of my buddies from the Corps turned me on to it," he told her. "Truth is, after I got back from The Storm this is about the only place that felt right to live in."

Monica looked at him curiously. "What do you mean?"

"I don't know if I can explain it," Zack said slowly. "Nothing that happens in boot camp prepares you for what war really is. We were there three months, that's all. But it was enough. Saw some bad stuff, real bad stuff. One day you're eating sand and breathing gas, watching yourself kill people you've never met, and the next day you're back home reading about yourself in *Time* magazine and eatin' a Big Mac. Too weird. Life changes that fast. You just don't feel like yourself anymore."

"I know the feeling," Monica sympathized.

"But of course, you talk to yourself, too." Sophie patted Monica's arm. "You must work on that, dear."

"Yes, and what brings you to these parts, Sophie?"

"That's privileged information, of course," she said in a hushed tone. "But I can tell you . . . when I'm finished with my work here . . ." Her voice broke. "Well, we must all make great sacrifices for truth."

"Do you have a family?" Monica asked.

Sophie looked a little agitated. "Well, that's privileged information, as well."

"What about you?" Zack asked Monica. "What's your story?"

"Well, actually, one morning I was wearing a beautiful coat, and by nightfall I was sleeping on the ground."

"Yeah, that happens," Pete spoke up. Until then he had been staring into space, and Monica wasn't sure if he was even listening.

"Is that what happened to you?" Monica asked, hoping desperately he'd talk more about himself.

"I don't have time for this," he said, wincing in pain as he tried to stand on his ailing feet. "I have to get to Colorado."

"Pete, you have to see a doctor," Monica said.

"No, you have to leave me alone—"

"Police! Everybody freeze!" Suddenly the station was ablaze with light and everyone was backing against the wall or running toward the exits. But the exits were blocked, and only a few escaped. "C'mon, move along. Let's go . . ." The police were herding everyone outside, and Monica felt herself being swept along with the rest of the crowd.

"Arms up, arms up," one officer ordered. "If you've got nothing to hide you've got nothing to worry about."

Out on the sidewalk, the officers frisked the men one by one as they filed by. Monica watched as they frisked Zack. He must have passed the test, whatever it was, because they waved him on. Then Pete stood before the same officer, shoulders slumped, almost like a limp puppet that could barely stand up on his own.

"Arms up," the officer ordered.

Pete just stood and looked at him.

"I said arms up," the officer repeated.

Monica stepped forward. "Uh, officer, he's not well," she said.

"I got a cold myself," the officer grumbled. "Arms up, pal."

Pete grudgingly raised his arms.

"Now the tote bag," the officer said, reaching for it.

"No." Pete clutched his bag closer to his side.

"Hey, I need some help here!" the officer called out.

Two more officers arrived at their partner's side.

"Pete, give it to them," Monica pleaded. Why couldn't he just cooperate? Whatever was in there couldn't be that important.

"No!" Pete said more loudly now.

"Just take it," the first officer said, and one of the others reached out for the bag.

"No!" Pete said again and pulled back.

One policeman thwacked Pete on the arm with his nightstick, while the other wrestled the bag away from Pete. Then the officer with the nightstick held Pete as the other pulled down the bag's zipper and emptied the contents onto the ground.

"No, please." Pete was sobbing now.

"You didn't have to do that," Zack said.

"Shut up," the officer returned as he sorted through the soiled clothing and other items: an old address book, a vinyl pouch with what looked like about thirty dollars in one-dollar bills, and a cylindrical metal container that hit the ground with a clank and rolled off toward the curb. Pete started screaming then, but no one could understand what he was saying.

Sophie pulled out a spiral notebook. "I want you to know I'm taking all your badge numbers," she said, beginning to write.

"Whaddya got?" one policeman asked the one kneeling on the ground rummaging through the bag.

"Nothing. Junk . . ." He noticed the round metal case then and reached over to pick it up. "Julie Taylor, D.O.D. 2/2/94," he read aloud. He turned to Pete then.

"My wife," Pete said, tears flowing freely down his face. "Her ashes. Julie."

After the shakedown, the station was off-limits for the night. So Monica decided to take her new friends to the underpass where she had spent the previous night. Pete was limping badly now, leaning on Zack and moaning in pain with every step. But he had his tote bag back, and that seemed to give him some comfort.

"It's not much, but at least it's out of the wind," Monica said as they looked for a flat piece of ground on which to sleep.

"Unless the wind changes," Pete said.

"Forty-four degrees," Sophie announced with a smile. "Only five more and we can go to the shelter."

"I'm not going to any shelter," Pete muttered, sitting down on the sidewalk to remove his shoes and rub his feet.

Zack reached into his boot and pulled out a bottle. He held it out to Pete. "This won't take the pain away, but you won't care as much about it."

Pete looked grateful for Zack's offer, but he shook his head. "No. Thanks."

Zack picked up an empty trash can and set it before them. "We're gonna need something to burn," he said and looked around him. He spotted a piece of broken fence and went to retrieve it, while Monica went on her own search. She was delighted to find a large cardboard box and began to drag it toward the trash can.

"Hey!" someone inside of the box yelled.

"Oh, dear!" Monica cried. "Please, I'm so sorry. I'm very sorry. Carry on."

She was still shaking from the episode a few moments later as Zack broke up the fence and placed the pieces into the trash can. Pete watched from a few feet away, while Sophie stood right beside the can and rubbed her hands together as though a fire were already blazing there.

"Oh, I just love a good fire," she said gleefully.

Zack turned to Monica. "You still got that lighter?" he asked.

"Right here." Monica pulled it out of her pocket and held it up, glad for something to contribute.

"Oh, we're going for a real fire," Sophie said, looking concerned. "I don't know. I don't know. Awfully risky."

Zack held up a piece of the fence while Monica tried to ignite it with the lighter, but the flame wouldn't catch.

"Maybe some paper or kindling or something," Pete suggested.

They surveyed the area once again, all eyes finally falling in unison on Sophie's shopping cart. It was quiet for a moment.

"You know," Sophie finally spoke, "there is that whole file from 1975 on J. Edgar Hoover I'd just as soon not be found in possession of under certain circumstances." She pulled it out and flipped through it nostalgically. She sighed. "This could blow the roof clean off of the Warren Commission, but . . ." She turned to Pete. "You just make sure it does some good, you hear? Get those little tootsies of yours nice and toasty, now."

Pete smiled. He seemed touched by Sophie's gesture. Monica certainly was.

"So, where were you in '63?" Sophie asked Pete.

"Nineteen sixty-three?" he mumbled.

"September, October . . ." she said, trying to help him out, then, "November?" she said more emphatically.

"Uh . . ." He frowned, trying to remember. "Fifth, sixth grade?"

Sophie handed the notebook to Zack, and he held it up to Monica, who then touched the lighter to it. The journal immediately caught fire. Monica sighed with relief. She was growing colder by the minute. She glanced up at the lighted temperature reading on the top of a nearby bank—forty-two degrees.

"Go on," Sophie encouraged Pete. "You were in fifth or sixth grade . . ."

And Sophie was able to do what neither Zack nor Monica could, no matter how hard they'd tried—open Pete up. As the four of them nestled close together in the night, they listened to Pete share his story. It took a while, but he finally got to the part about Julie, the part Monica knew had had a huge impact on his life.

". . . She always used to tease me, 'cause she wore a wedding ring and I didn't. Truth is, we could only afford one ring. We were gonna buy me one someday. But . . ." He paused. "I'm kinda glad now that we didn't. I might've had to pawn it."

"What happened to Julie?" Monica prodded gently.

"She died last year," he said. "Savings and loan went down, took my business along with it. Lost our health insurance, and a few weeks later Julie started feeling sick, but . . ." He stopped and seemed to be in pain. "She put off going to the doctor until one of us could find a job and get coverage again. By the time anybody knew it was cancer, it was too late. I stayed home to take care of her, threw a lot of medical bills in the drawer, and by February I'd lost my house and my wife." He sighed. "She got me off of booze. Haven't taken a drink since she said, 'Yes, I'll marry you.' She had faith enough for both of us—always talked about going to Colorado and starting over again. I promised I'd go, even if it was without her. So I got in my van and headed west. And then it broke down. And now it's gone . . ." He shrugged and sat there with his head bowed.

They all sat quietly for a moment. It was Sophie who broke the awkward silence.

"There but for the grace of God go I," she said sincerely.

Monica glanced at the temperature again. Forty-one degrees.

It couldn't have been that much later, though it seemed like hours, until they looked up one more time to see the temperature flashing thirty-nine degrees. A murmur of cheers rumbled through the underpass as everyone began to gather up their belongings.

"Hallelujah! Put a hot brick in the sheets, honey, Sophie's coming home!" Sophie began to push her cart after the others heading toward the shelter.

"You ever spent a night in the shelter?" Zack asked Monica.

"No."

"Brace yourself. And stick with Sophie."

Monica nodded and began to follow Zack, who was following Sophie. But a quick glance back revealed that Pete hadn't budged from where he sat on the ground.

"Pete?" she called out to him. "Are you coming?"

He shook his head. "I told you. I don't go to shelters."

"Maybe tonight you'd better make an exception," she told him.

"You ever seen a guy lay carpet down?" he asked.

Monica shook her head.

"Well, there's this big metal thing called a power stretcher. You get down on all fours and put the carpet where you want it and then you slam your knees into steel about six thousand times a day to nail the carpet to the floor. After twelve hours or so, you don't have a knee anymore, just pain." He had managed to get one shoe off and was loosening the heel of the other. "The only thing that could take it away was Julie. She had the most beautiful hands in the world." He paused. "She was the last person to ever touch me."

Monica watched as Pete attempted to rub his damaged feet. She just couldn't imagine touching those sores, those open wounds. What if . . .

"That's okay," Pete said. "That wasn't a hint."

"If you stay out here tonight, you may die."

"So?" Pete summed up, in that one word, exactly how he felt about himself and his life.

"You still have to take Julie to Colorado," Monica said softly.

Pete's expression softened. He carefully pulled his shoes back onto his feet. Monica offered him her arm, and the two caught up with Sophie and Zack.

The admission line into the Haven of Rest Shelter snaked around the block and across the street into the next block. Everyone had arrived at exactly the same time. A man in a long coat walked down the line and finally approached Pete.

"You need something? Booze, cigarettes, shampoo?"

Pete shook his head.

"It's ten percent cheaper outside." The man opened up his coat to reveal the merchandise attached to the lining. "Inside, when the temperature goes higher, so do my prices."

"Get lost, Ox," Zack said.

"Hey, I got something for you, too, Marine," Ox returned. He pulled a whiskey bottle out of the lining of his jacket. Zack stared at it. "How much?" he asked.

"How about that ring?" Ox said with a smirk.

"Not on your life," Zack said quickly.

"Just a matter of time," Ox said confidently. "Just a matter of time."

The foursome finally arrived at the head of the line. A young woman stood at the door. She put up her hand before they could move past her. "Sorry, folks, this is a families-only shelter."

"What?" Pete exclaimed in disbelief.

"We're a familiy," Sophie said indignantly, motioning to Monica, Zack, and Pete. "These are my children."

The woman eyed Zack's dark skin suspiciously and opened her mouth to say something.

"He's from my second marriage," Sophie told her quickly.

The woman shook her head. Then suddenly an African-American woman in a tattered gray coat hurried up to Sophie. Monica could have cried with relief. Tess.

"Sophie, honey, how are you?" Tess exclaimed, taking the homeless woman's arm. "I haven't seen you in ages! Just look how your babies have grown! Isn't this one a beauty?" She pinched Monica's cheek as if she were a five-year-old.

"Why yes, yes she is," Sophie replied. "Who would have thought—all those years of braces paid off!"

The woman shrugged and let them through. "Men to the left, women upstairs!" she barked.

Zack took Pete's arm to guide him up the stairs. "Hold on, my man. Excellent accommodations await. Just like Desert Storm, but without the sand."

Monica started upstairs. "Tess, what a relief! Where have you been?" But when she turned around, Tess was gone.

And Sophie wasn't behind her either. She was arguing with the young woman at the door. Monica could hear their raised voices.

"I just can't sleep upstairs," Sophie said.

"I don't care if you sleep, I just need you up there," the woman replied impatiently.

"I can't. Where's Tom?"

"Tom's night off," she told Sophie. "Upstairs or outside. Your choice."

"Do you have a room up there with no windows?" Sophie asked.

Monica tentatively approached the anxious woman. "-We'll go upstairs," she said, taking hold of Sophie's arm. "Come on, Sophie." Monica tugged on her arm. "It'll be okay."

Sophie reluctantly followed her, and the two women found a couple of beds in one corner of a large room. The old woman immediately lay down and tied herself to her bed with pieces of her underclothing. She was asleep in minutes.

Monica sat on the edge of her bed, removed her sneakers, and rubbed her tired feet. She thought of Pete downstairs and wondered if he were sleeping or lying on his bed awake and thinking of Julie.

Pete clutched his tote bag as he lay down on the lumpy mattress. To think that he had come so close to losing all that he had left of his dear wife. He shuddered to think of it. He was too tired to even remove his shoes, so in spite of the constant din of loud snores and idle chatter, he was able to fall asleep.

He awoke sometime later to hear anguished screams from a bed across the room. He sat up and peered into the darkness at the thrashing figure. Zack—what was wrong with him? Pete hurried across the room.

"What's the matter, man?" Pete asked, shaking him. "Wake up, wake up."

"I can't move!" Zack cried. "I can't move!"

"Hey, you're all right," Pete assured him. "Wake up."

Suddenly Zack's eyes flew open, and he stared at Pete in terror. "Man, I hate those things," he said.

"What was going on in there?" Pete asked.

"My usual nightmare," Zack said, still shaking. "I'm in the desert in the middle of a fire fight. And everybody knows there's land mines all over the place, but nobody knows where they are. And I know if I move, I'm gonna die. And I know I'm gonna die if I don't move." He paused and looked at Pete. "You wouldn't understand."

"Oh, yeah, I think I would," Pete said quickly. "But you're having the wrong kind of dreams, man. You can't waste your time dreaming about the past. You gotta stick to dreamin' about the future."

"But being a marine's the one thing I did best," Zack protested. "I belonged to something. I mean, that's who I was."

"And who are you now?" Pete asked.

Zack didn't answer right away. "I don't know," he said finally and looked down.

"I know," Pete said. "You're a guy who can't even think about next week 'cuz you're just trying to get through today. Thinkin' like that," he said pointing to his head, "that's what's going to keep you on the streets. You gotta have a dream bigger than where you're going to sleep tonight." He paused. "You got any family?"

"I—I got a brother, but we don't talk." He looked up at Pete. "I don't talk."

"Next quarter you get man ... you put it in the phone." Pete slapped him on the shoulder, then headed back to his bed.

Pete sat back down on his bed and reached around for his tote bag. He began to panic. Where was it? He got down on his knees and looked under the bed, thinking he might have accidentally kicked it under there. Back up on top of the bed now. Under the sheets. He'd left it right in the middle of his bed. He remembered. It was gone. Someone had taken it.

"Hey!" he yelled. "Hey! Wake up! Who took it? I know someone's got it. Come on! My bag! Please! Please!" He began to run from bed to bed, waking up each occupant and throwing the covers off to look for the missing bag.

Two guards appeared at his side then, and one took him by the shoulders. "Come on, man," he said. "Go back to bed."

With amazing strength, Pete shook him off. "No! No! They stole it. My bag. Somebody's got my bag! Oh, Julie ..." He crumpled to the floor now, sobbing hysterically.

The guards glared down at him. "You're waking everybody up!" one of them said. "Either go back to bed, or outside!"

"No! No! Not until I get it back."

"Let's go, buddy," the other guard said, and the two of them lifted him to his feet. "You're outta here."

He couldn't stop sobbing as they dragged him down the stairs and pushed him out the door. He fell face first onto the cold, hard pavement.

He lay in a heap on the sidewalk and cried until he could cry no longer. Then, exhausted, he just lay there whimpering for a few moments. Finally, he found himself stumbling to his feet and down the sidewalk. The temperature had fallen a few more degrees, and after he'd walked about a block, he spotted a group of men standing around a fire in a trash can, passing a bottle in a bag back and forth between them. He moved toward them.

"State your business," an older man growled at him.

"What's that?" Pete asked, pointing to the bag.

"First sip's free," the man said. "Then you gotta pay."

He handed the bottle to Pete. It had been so long. He hesitated, then closed his eyes and tipped his head back, taking a long gulp.

"I got a good pair of shoes here." He pointed to his feet. "They'll last a long time." Pete took another gulp, while the man bent down to check out his shoes.

The young woman opened the front door for Monica, and she stepped out into the cold.

"Now, if you walk out, you can't come back in," the woman told her in a stern tone. "Those are the rules. This ain't no revolving door hotel."

Monica nodded. "I know."

The door slammed shut behind her then, and she shoved her hands into her pockets and looked around. She'd recognized Pete's voice immediately when he started screaming, but the female guard wouldn't let Monica leave her room until she finally convinced her it was an emergency, that someone needed her.

She started walking now until she finally came to the underpass where she saw Pete curled up in a corner, asleep, barefoot, and clutching an empty liquor bottle to his chest. Monica watched him for some time before slumping down

PETE (GREGORY HARRISON) SLEEPS WHILE
MONICA QUESTIONS GOD

at his side. She rocked back and forth to keep her blood flowing.

"Oh, Father, why have You forsaken me?" she whispered into the night. "What did I do wrong? Why are You punishing me? Why have You taken away who I am, *what* I am? I don't . . ." She let the tears fall freely. "I don't even feel like an angel anymore."

She felt a presence and looked up to see Tess standing over her. "You don't need to be an angel to give that man what he needs right now," Tess said.

"Oh, Tess," Monica moaned. "I thought . . . I thought . . ."

"Has God ever forsaken you, Monica?" Tess asked, stroking Monica's hair. "He told you He wouldn't, and He never has. Never. Just because you feel invisible, doesn't mean you are. Never give up, baby."

Monica scrambled to her feet and threw her arms around her mentor.

"Maybe you know now how it feels to be forgotten, stripped of everything that you think makes you, you. Hmmm? What did you do right now? Did you ask the Father for food? Did you ask Him to make you warmer?"

Monica shook her head. "I asked to be . . . remembered. I needed to know that I still mattered."

"So does he." Tess pointed to Pete. "You've been a caseworker treating him like a case. But he's a man. He needs to know he can still make a difference. And you . . . you need to let him."

"How do I do that?" Monica asked.

"First of all, realize that this has not been a punishment, sweetheart," Tess said with a smile. "It's been a lesson in pride."

Monica bowed her head, crying harder now. She felt so ashamed, of her own shallowness, of the selfish side that had emerged when her comforts were compromised.

"Shame brings you down," Tess went on. "But true humility only lifts you higher." She gestured to Pete, then was gone again.

Monica looked at him. She smiled when she saw a basin of water and a towel folded up next to him. She knelt beside him and removed the bottle from his arms. He awakened then and seemed almost disappointed to find himself still alive.

"Hello, Pete," Monica said softly. "I want to ask a favor of you."

Pete motioned to the cardboard box Monica almost nabbed from the homeless person the night before. "Sorry," he snapped back. "I've already got somebody in the guest room." He rolled over onto his stomach, tucking his head under his forearms.

"No, I just . . . I just want you to listen to me for a moment, please," she pleaded. Somehow she knew this was her last chance to reach him.

Pete sat up, seeming to sense her seriousness.

"You need to know. I'm—I'm an angel," she said.

A small smile spread across his face.

"I know it sounds crazy . . ."

"Not around here," he said.

"Well, it's hard to explain, but proving it to you doesn't even matter to me right now. But please let me apologize to you. I was getting awfully . . . big for my wings, I guess . . . and I needed to learn a few things about being an angel."

He stared at her, listening.

"Please . . . there is something I need to do. I *want* to do. It's what I need to do to remember who I am."

Monica took the waiting towel and dipped it into the basin of warm water. Then she lifted Pete's disfigured left foot

MONICA WASHES THE FEET OF PETE (GREGORY HARRISON)

and held it gently against her bent knee. She washed it thoroughly, carefully laid it down, and then moved on to his right foot.

"I don't know why these things have happened to you, but they are not because of anything you have done, Pete," Monica assured him. "And I confess that somewhere in my heart, I thought maybe you *had* done something to get here. Will you forgive me?"

Pete looked uncomfortable, as if he didn't know what to say.

"Please," she said. "It matters."

"I . . . I forgive you," he said.

His face was suddenly illuminated in the darkness, and Monica's rags were transformed into a flowing white dress. Gone were the tattered clothes of the homeless woman, and she was instead surrounded by light. Together, they looked down, astonished to see that Pete's feet were now miraculously as soft and smooth as a newborn baby's. The sores and blisters that had caused him such anguish and pain had vanished.

Pete looked at her in awe.

"God loves you, Pete Taylor," Monica said confidently. "I have failed you, but He will not. He wants you to know that He is going to take you … and Julie … to Colorado. He will walk with you all the way, but you must take the first step." She motioned to his feet. "I guess that's what I was here for all along."

Monica managed to smile through the tears that stained her face. Pete nodded and returned her smile.

Monica wore clean clothes the following morning when she walked back into the mission. Zack sat at a table at the rear of the main room, leaning back in a chair and aimlessly spinning his insignia ring. Tess, in her threadbare coat, studied a nearby bulletin board, while Sophie studied Tess. Monica couldn't help overhearing as she walked slowly across the room.

"Now where exactly did we meet again?" Sophie asked with a frown.

Tess turned to her. "Well, do you remember when you lived on South Cherry Street?"

Sophie's face fell. "That's privileged information," she said.

"I know it is, honey," Tess said. "But I've got high-level security clearance. And I'm telling you that nobody blames you for closing up shop and hightailing it outta there. As a matter of fact, I'm the one who gave you the ride, remember?"

Sophie beamed. "The cab driver!"

"Got my own rig now," Tess continued. "You oughta see it. Nice, big old red thing . . . but anyway, I'm here to tell you, Sophie, that it's safe for you to go home now, and no man's gonna lift a hand to you again."

Sophie frowned. "You never know what direction it comes from," she said. "Sometimes from the underpass, sometimes from the grassy knoll."

Tess took a flyer off the bulletin board and handed it to Sophie. "You can relax now, honey." She put an arm around the homeless woman's shoulder. "This just got put up today. Your kids and your grandkids are looking for you. They miss you. They want to take care of you. They want to protect you."

Sophie clutched the flyer to her chest.

Tess began to lead her into the hall. "Come on, let's go make a phone call."

Monica was headed toward Zack when she happened to spot the wheeler-dealer named Ox from the day before sitting at a nearby table drinking something from a styrofoam cup.

He beckoned to her with his finger. "Come on over, baby, and sit by me," he said. "How'd you get so clean, woman?"

Monica ignored his question. "Excuse me, Mr. . . . Ox, I believe you have something that doesn't belong to you."

He laughed. "I got a lot of things like that, baby. Which one you talkin' about?"

"A rather . . . cylindrical tubelike thing. Metal. I believe it was . . . *appropriated* last night. Maybe in the men's dormitory upstairs?" She stared at him until he began to squirm.

Finally, he opened his coat and pulled the container out of a large tacked-on pocket. "I'm positive I've never seen it," he said coyly. "But if I did happen to come across it, what would it be worth to you?"

"Well, I don't have anything to offer," she hedged, searching her mind for some way to make a deal with Ox.

Ox leered at her. "Oh yeah? You sure—"

Suddenly Zack appeared at Monica's side. He held his Marine ring out to Ox.

Ox nodded smugly. "I always knew you and me, we'd do some business."

"The ring for the can, Ox," Zack said. "And a quarter."

"A quarter?" Ox dug into his pocket and pulled out a quarter, then dropped it into Zack's hand. "Whatever."

Zack dropped his ring into the con man's palm. Monica knew it was a huge step for him—a symbol of truly moving out of the past and into the present. Ox handed the metal can to Monica.

"God bless you," she said softly.

Monica and Pete finally stood together on top of the Colorado mountain Julie had loved. As Monica nodded, he poured the ashes into the wind that immediately carried them away. When he turned to smile at Monica, she was gone. Pete stood on the mountain alone, knowing full well that he had been not only touched by an angel, but touched by God. And he knew that no matter what happened in the future, he would never be the same. He would never really be alone again. ∼

Response to the Show

Roma Downey

This was probably the most touching of all of our shows. All the extras were found in a homeless shelter, and they were so grateful to earn a salary and receive two hot meals a day. We were coming up to Christmastime, and everybody felt that we were contributing in some way, giving something back. We did a huge drive for toys and clothes and took them over to the shelter. It really affected everybody, and I think the message the show was giving the rest of the country was felt very profoundly by the cast and crew. And the message was: "There but for the grace of God go you or I." We all counted our blessings that Christmas.

There were times in that huge railway station and in the cold when we were freezing. But at least we knew that between shots we could take refuge in a warm trailer. It moved us to do something for those less fortunate than ourselves.

Marion Ross—Sophie

When I played the homeless woman, we were shooting at Christmastime. That made it the sweetest, deepest

Christmas in years. Here we were with "no place in the inn." We hired homeless people and many of them made enough money to get a van or a car and a Christmas dinner with lobster and steak. Some of the actors donated their salaries and gave a gift or cash bonus for every child. All of a sudden I knew what Christmas was really about—it was about helping someone with no place to go, someone who had no place in the inn.

As I was walking around in my costume, a priest came out of a church and said hello to me. His greeting meant so much that now I try to say hello to people I see on the street. I know that priest thought I was a homeless person.

I'm so proud to work with Martha Williamson because she's done what so many in this town have tried to do. She's really tapped into a tremendous need, and she's asked everyone connected to the show to be the best they can be. The whole town is about trying to get a hit series—that's what the business is. Martha did it with this unspeakable subject. You don't talk about angels and being good.

FROM VIEWERS

I want to tell you what *Touched by an Angel* did for me and my relationship with my brother . . . a majority of the time he is on the street, in a V.A. hospital, or jail. . . . I didn't want to be bothered with him coming to our home. Then Saturday night . . . what this episode was about . . . the homeless . . . it made me look at myself.

There was a pride and selfishness in my heart. I called my brother and asked him to forgive me and he did and you know, for the first time in my life, I told my brother that I loved him. I just wanted you to know how much the country needs this show.

Columbus, Ohio

My class recently viewed *Touched by an Angel*. The video showed me that all poor people did not deserve it. Most become poor because of circumstances beyond their control. . . . The program opened my eyes and inspired me.

So many times you hear about the poor and hungry in other countries that you forget about the poor and hungry in your own country. I hope this program will give many other people in our country a better perspective about the poor and make them realize they are very lucky to have a home to go to and people to love and care for them.

The foot-washing section of the show hit close to home. It showed me to always be humble towards others, superiors and inferiors, no matter what happens.

High school students in Jackson, Michigan

CHAPTER 4

An Unexpected Snow

Megan: "After a while, you spend enough nights alone
and you go to too many other people's weddings and
baby showers. You spend too many holidays at other
people's houses, and you want just a little piece of their
happiness for yourself, you know? Just for a while. Just
so you can say someday that somebody wanted me.
Somebody thought I was worth it."

The Story Behind the Story

An Unexpected Snow" was our first season
Thanksgiving episode. Our airdate schedule was
so erratic and unpredictable then that it actually
aired in December. Nevertheless, it was the first *Touched*
episode to yield a noticeable increase in viewer response.

In the earlier "Tough Love," the brilliant performance of
Phylicia Rashad as an alcoholic journalist inspired quite a lot
of audience mail. It was our first indication that we were really
on to something. It is still one of our most requested "repeat"
shows. But the sheer volume and passion of the letters we

received after "Unexpected Snow" convinced us that people were not only watching the show, they were actually making changes in their lives because of what they saw.

The twist in this episode is about adultery, but the story is really about loss of hope, the belief that there can be nothing better for you than what you have now. As a single woman in my twenties and thirties, I spent countless hours with girlfriends trying to figure out what we were doing wrong. Why couldn't we find a satisfying relationship? Why couldn't we keep the ones we'd found? How many times did we sit in a restaurant and say to each other: "Honey, you deserve better than that guy"?

In "Unexpected Snow," Megan, "the other woman," reveals the heartbreaking fear that every human being has known sometime or another: This is all there is, there is nothing better for me. I don't deserve anything better anyway, so I'll just take what I can get for as long as it lasts. A little love (or money, or respect, or success) is better than none at all.

When we desire a piece of someone else's happiness instead of our own, we have traded our dreams for theirs. And suddenly they are not our dreams at all. And that is the beginning of hopelessness.

A few years ago, I decided to remind myself of what *my* dreams were—all of them. The one from elementary school about being a famous singer. The one from high school about fitting into a size 8. The one from college about writing Broadway musicals and being the toast of New York. The one about running into my old boyfriends and making them realize what a great deal they were missing now. The one about going to Paris. And taking piano lessons again. The one about catching up on all my thank-you notes. And, of course, the one about being loved for who I am.

I wrote down all the dreams on a piece of paper. I discovered how many of them I had simply stopped hoping for. Just like Megan, I had been willing to settle for shadows of my dreams because I was afraid to hope for more. Megan learns the lesson I did: When our dreams begin to die, so do we. When we share our dreams with God, He won't laugh and say, "Well, good luck." As a matter of fact, God will take our dreams more seriously than we do, because He knows no compromise. He doesn't deal in pieces of happiness and shadows of dreams. He will ask more of us than we ask of ourselves, but He will return more to us than we could ever hope or imagine ourselves.

Many people have asked about the title, "Unexpected Snow." The title was taken from an extraordinary experience shared with me one day on the set by our legendary supervising producer and mainstay Jon Andersen. Only months earlier, he had lost his son in a tragic mountain climbing accident. The memorial for "Eazy" was held on a warm spring day in a garden in the Canadian Rockies. Several hundred people attended the service, and as it ended, inexplicably and as if on cue, it began to snow. A soft, light dusting of snowflakes floated silently to the ground. And when everyone left the meadow, the snow simply stopped. Jon said it was as if God's presence had literally descended gently and reassuringly on his friends and family. It was their "unexpected snow," a quiet, everyday miracle that reminded a grieving father of God's presence in the midst of hopelessness, and of His promise of new hope when a dream has died.

For all of us who have lost or forgotten our dreams, we offered "An Unexpected Snow."

—M. W.

AN UNEXPECTED SNOW

TELEPLAY AND STORY BY MARTHA WILLIAMSON

When two women forge a friendship only to discover a man in the middle, it takes the hospitality of angels to orchestrate a Thanksgiving that will live in their memories forever.

*T*he air blew briskly through the canyon, and the sun shone brightly in the brilliant blue sky on the afternoon of Thanksgiving eve. Tess and Monica stood together on a rocky hillside, surveying the mountains in the distance and the rough terrain beneath their feet. Below them, a two-lane road came winding down through the canyon pass. The landscape around them lay empty for miles, and Monica searched for just the right spot to position the house that would serve as a backdrop for her next assignment.

"I don't care what you decide to do, angel girl," Tess told Monica. "Just make the walk to the front door a short one."

"Oh, but a long driveway is so much more dramatic," Monica said, clasping her hands together and picturing it in her mind.

"Honey, there's plenty of drama ahead, driveway or no driveway."

Monica frowned. "She's late," she said as she gazed down the narrow road behind them.

Tess shook her head. "No such thing as late. Destiny picks its own time."

"What do I do when it happens?" Monica asked.

"Destiny doesn't happen, it arrives." Tess smiled. "And when it does, you either batten down the hatches and wait for it to blow over, or you swing open the gates and invite it in to supper."

"I wish it had a way of showing itself, so she'd know what she's dealing with." Monica sighed. She couldn't help feeling sorrow when she thought about the pain her next assignment was about to encounter. All of her assignments seemed to face their most painful difficulties in life just as Monica was about to appear on the scene. That was her role—to walk with them through the pain.

"Then it wouldn't be destiny," Tess replied wisely.

Of course. "And I wouldn't have a job," Monica said.

"Girl, you've come a long way." Her mentor nodded approval, then cocked her head as they heard a motor chugging up the mountain road. "Hark!" she cried out, as though announcing glad tidings.

Monica looked at her teasingly. "Hark?"

Tess shrugged. "Sometimes I miss the old days."

They looked down to see a late model white sedan bouncing up the road in one direction while a red car careened down the narrow road in the opposite direction. The white one seemed to be taking the turns a little too fast, and the red one seemed to be taking up more than its share of the barely two-lane road.

Suddenly, the white car swerved around a hairpin turn heading straight into the other car. Both drivers jerked their vehicles violently in opposite directions, sideswiping each other and forcing one into a ditch and the other through a fence.

Monica and Tess watched from the hilltop as the driver of the red car threw open the door and scrambled out of her car, her pretty face contorted by an angry grimace. The attractive brunette looked as if she might be in her late thirties. She wore a long gray coat and black pumps. Furious, she immediately started punching the buttons on her cell phone, listening, then cursing, obviously unable to reach anyone.

The other driver climbed out of her car, looking a little dazed. Tendrils of blond curly hair flew out from her head in every direction. Dressed in light-colored jeans, a white jacket, and casual brown loafers, the woman in her early thirties looked ready for a weekend in the country rather than a date with destiny.

"Operator, thank God," the first woman cried into the tiny receiver. "There's been an accid . . . hello? Hello?" she shouted again, then, with a look of disgust, pushed the antenna back into the phone.

"Are you all right?" she called across the highway as the other driver stumbled toward her.

"That depends," the blond woman shot back. "Were you calling an ambulance or a lawyer?"

"I *am* a lawyer."

"Figures," the younger woman said as she began to cross the road. "Drive to kill, right?"

"Now wait a minute," the other countered, "you almost ran right into me."

The angels exchanged glances as the banter continued.

"Which one is Megan?" Monica asked.

"It's the nature girl," Tess said. "Susana is the lawyer."

Monica smiled slightly as she tapped Tess on the shoulder and pointed behind them. Suddenly, there appeared before them two iron gates and an elegant brick driveway leading up to the top of the hill.

"Very nice," Tess said, and the two of them began to walk down the hill toward the bickering Megan and Susana.

"Hello," Monica greeted cheerfully as she and Tess approached the two women. "Had a wee bit of a scrape, did you?"

The two women stopped arguing to stare at Monica and Tess.

"Do you have a phone?" Susana asked in an impatient tone. "My cellular won't hold a signal."

"Oh, that's a pity," Tess said. "There's not a phone around here for miles."

"Is either of you hurt?" Monica asked, looking them up and down.

"I'm fine," Megan answered, then turned to Susana. "How about you?"

Susana looked surprised that Megan would even think to ask. "Oh, I'm fine. Just a little . . . I'm fine. Where's the nearest gas station?"

"Right next to the nearest phone," Tess said, unable to hide a smile.

But Susana was understandably frustrated. "Well, this is great. Just great."

"Yes, it is, isn't it?" Monica said. "We were hoping to have some company for the holidays."

"You live out here?" Megan asked in a slightly shocked voice.

"Well, we're sort of . . . house-sitting for a friend," Monica explained. "He's got a house just through those gates. It's going to be dark soon—"

"Does he have a car?" Susana asked abruptly. "I've got to get out of here."

"If he has a car, I have as much right to it as you," Megan demanded.

"*I* had the right of way, lady," Susana said fiercely.

"Right of way?" Megan cried. "Are you out of—"

"You were barreling down—"

"Ladies, please!" Monica interrupted. "Look, we have no car and no phone. But we do have good food and warm beds and a hearth where you're welcome for the night." She paused. "Tomorrow is Thanksgiving. Let's be thankful you lived to see it."

"Amen, sister," Tess agreed.

The chastened women seemed to calm down. Megan sighed and returned to her car to get her duffel bag, while Susana pulled a small suitcase on rollers out of the backseat of hers. The four women exchanged names, and then Susana went back to trying to get through to someone on her cellular as the travelers reluctantly followed Monica and Tess through the gate and up the steep tree-lined driveway.

"Is someone expecting you for Thanksgiving?" Monica asked Megan, who walked just slightly behind her.

"No," she answered quietly. "I thought I was spending it with my boyfriend, but . . ." She forced a smile. ". . . plans changed. I was on my way back to the city. Don't know how I ended up on that road."

Behind them Susana wove back and forth across the road, frantically attempting to capture the elusive cell that would bring a taxi or tow truck to her rescue. "No service," she said, reading the phone. "No service. 'Roaming.' I *am* roaming!" Abruptly she stopped and glared down at the receiver, then held it to her ear. But her anger was preempted by a momentary flash of terror—she screamed as a large creature thrashed through the bushes beside her. There, a mere foot away, stood a llama, staring curiously at her.

"Now I've seen everything!" she said, making no attempt to hide her exasperation.

"That's a llama," Tess said calmly.

"And I suppose you're Doctor Doolittle?" Susana tried her phone again and groaned. "No service."

"The llama is a very sensitive creature," Tess said. "He seems to like you."

Susana stared at the animal. "What can he do?" she asked.

"He just is," Tess told her.

Susana frowned, but they were almost to the front door of the house now, a French Norman chateau, the creation of Monica's miraculous ingenuity and elegant taste. The beautiful home was fashioned with counterpane and brick and sported two turrets. Scurrying through the front yard were birds of various sorts: ducks, a pheasant, a turkey. In spite of the free-ranging livestock, the grounds were immaculate and the fragrant gardens were lush with bluebells, heather, and climbing roses.

"What is that?" Megan asked, sniffing. "Cedar?"

Monica nodded. "Cedar in the hearth, fire in the soul," she said.

"I love the smell of cedar," Megan said, breathing deeply. Monica smiled at her. "Yes."

"What is that?" Susana asked in a high-pitched voice as she pointed at the bird in the front yard, staring at her. "A turkey?"

"Yes," Tess warned. "But don't get too attached."

The four women climbed the front steps and moved through the door into the entryway, where the guests set their bags down on an Oriental rug. The home was as beautifully appointed as its gardens, with huge windows and plenty of sunshine to illuminate the Victorian portraits, antiques, books, and treasures that filled every square foot.

"Your room is the first one on the top floor," Monica told Megan. "And yours," she said, turning to Susana, "is at the top of the stairs."

"Excuse me." Susana stopped everyone as they began to move in different directions. "Before we all split up, I must insist on seeing some form of identification from you," she said to Megan.

Monica wasn't prepared for this request. "Do you really think that's necessary?" she asked.

Susana glanced at Megan for support, but the other woman didn't say anything. "We have been involved in an accident," Susana began, "and whether or not we can report it, I think we should follow some sort of protocol."

Monica began to wonder if Susana's background as an attorney was going to make life difficult for them the next few days.

"Excuse *me*," Tess said, "but we are all ladies of good character here, and *I* must insist that business matters be left outside at the door. Now those cars aren't going anywhere tonight and neither are you, so you girls just make yourself at home. Whatever you find you may use. Dinner's at eight.

Please dress appropriately. And bring a new word to share with the others."

Susana and Megan stared at her.

"Excuse me?" Megan said.

"A new word?" Susana said. "What is this, a game?"

"Yes," Tess replied, smiling.

Megan climbed the stairs to her room at the top, a cozy romantic loft with fresh roses in a cut crystal bowl and a candle burning on the dresser. The bed was covered with a floral comforter, and a crocheted coverlet was folded at the foot. The accessory pillows at the headboard were plump and plentiful. She placed her bag carefully onto a handsomely weathered steamer trunk, retrieved a few small items, and placed them on top of the dresser. She opened the left door of the mahogany armoire. There, on a petit point hanger, hung an exquisite knit jacket and pants outfit with a belt and coordinating pair of shoes. She took the hanger off the doweling rod and held the outfit in front of her, then stepped in front of the mirror. Megan would never have chosen it for herself, but still, it brought a smile to her face. She laid the outfit down on the bed and returned to the dresser.

Then she opened a zippered case and removed a brush, curling iron, perfume bottle, and a small double-sided enamel picture frame. Megan opened the frame slowly, looking down at her precious photographs. On the left side was a formal portrait of her boyfriend Jack in a suit and tie. On the right was a picture of Megan and Jack in matching sweaters seated at a table in a small cafe. They were laughing, and his arm was around her shoulders.

She looked at it with longing. They had been so happy at dinner that night at an out-of-the-way place in the country. It was just a few months after Megan had met Jack. He and several of his colleagues had arrived at her studio to get a portrait taken for their company's annual report. He had flirted relentlessly, and after several telephone calls and three dozen roses, she finally agreed to meet him for lunch. That was over a year ago now. She was about to set the frame on the bedside table but reconsidered, closed it up, and tossed it back into her bag. Then she sighed and set it back on the table.

Megan shook her head. This was crazy. What was she doing here? She walked to the window and looked down into the garden below.

A man in a white suit, shirt, and shoes stood beside the llama, feeding it something from the palm of his hand.

Monica passed through the enormous kitchen, with its hand-painted tiles, polished copper pots, and wood-burning stove, and then she went out the back door. She moved down the stairs into the garden and came up behind Andrew and the llama.

The presence of the angel of death was more than a surprise. What had brought him to the chateau on this night before Thanksgiving?

"Andrew?" she said hesitantly. She knew her voice betrayed her worry.

He turned around with a smile, easing her concern somewhat. "It's okay," he said. "It's Thanksgiving, and I've got the time off. I can't think of anybody I'd rather spend it with."

"But we're working," Monica reminded him. It wasn't that she didn't want him around; it just felt terribly awkward to her. "I don't know—it's risky, your being here. Tess won't like it."

"I could help."

"I can't have the angel of death running through some-body's destiny," she told him.

"Who knows?" he said, his eyes twinkling. "Maybe I'm supposed to be a part of it."

Dinner that evening was light; homemade chicken soup and biscuits. Megan was surprised when the man she'd seen earlier in the garden with Monica strode into the parlor and sat down at the table with them.

"This is Andrew, a family friend," Tess explained. "He's just passing through, and I prevailed upon him to join us for the weekend."

"Weekend?" Susana said. "I'm sure you're planning a lovely Thanksgiving and all, but I plan to be gone first thing in the morning one way or the other."

"What a shame," Andrew said with a smile in Susana's direction.

"I'm meeting my husband, actually," she went on. "He's probably worried sick about me. We've never spent a holi-day apart." She eyed Andrew, who was taking a bite out of his biscuit. "Maybe you could give me a lift in the morning?"

"A lift?" Andrew looked confused and turned to Tess.

"The morning's a long way off," Monica chimed in quickly.

"Right, Susana," Tess said. "We usually end our meal with a new word. And I'm ready to hear yours."

Susana thought for a moment. "Quittance."

"Quittance?" Monica repeated with a frown.

"Quittance." Andrew nodded. "I use the word all the time."

"Oh, what does it mean?" Megan asked.

"I don't know." Andrew shrugged. "I just say it and people nod as if they understand."

Everyone laughed.

"Quittance: a repayment, reparations," Susana said. "Satisfaction of payment."

"That's not a new word for you," Megan said. "That's legalese. That's cheating."

"I don't cheat," Susana snarled.

Everyone was quiet for a moment, and then Megan thought of a word that would surely put Susana in her place. She was actually pleased with herself for thinking of it.

"I've got a word," she said.

"Excuse me?" Tess said.

"Rodomontade," she repeated. "Hot air. Pretension. Bull." She eyed Susana across the table. "You know what, Counselor? You've been working too hard."

Susana let her fork clatter onto her plate. She wiped her mouth with her napkin, then stood up. "You may be right. I'm going to bed. The dinner was very nice," she said, nodding to Tess. Then she turned and walked away from the table.

Megan watched Monica and Tess exchange a glance. Okay, maybe she'd pushed things too far, but right now she didn't even care. She eased herself away from the table and stood up.

"I'm going for a walk," she said.

Later in the parlor, Monica and Tess sat across from one another in matching gray armchairs. On the coffee table between them was an antique game—an old cage filled with small numbered balls. Inside of each ball was a folded slip of paper with a question written on it. Monica turned the old crank to rotate the cage, then pulled out a ball. She grinned at Tess, then read from the piece of paper.

"Describe your first love." She sighed, then threw Tess a pleading look.

"How can I make a difference here? I've never been in love, you know, Tess. I don't know anything about romance."

"This is not a destiny of romance, Monica," Tess said. "This is a moment of truth. And love is only part of the truth. This a house where deception cannot live. We are nurturing a friendship that won't last long. But it will be based on truth. And the truth shall set them free."

The next morning, after a shower that helped wake her, Megan went downstairs to where Tess, Monica, and Susana were sharing a light breakfast of croissants and fresh fruit out on the deck in the backyard. The lady lawyer was dressed in a suit and looked more ready for a deposition than a day in the mountains. Her purse hung over one shoulder, and she seemed eager to take to the road.

"Good morning," Monica greeted Megan. "How did you sleep?"

"Great, thank you," she answered. "Actually, really great." She gestured to her outfit. "I found this outfit. I hope you don't mind . . ."

Monica smiled. "That's what it was there for."

Susana looked up from her coffee. "She loaned you some clothes?" she asked, a tinge of jealousy in her voice.

"I left some for you, too," Monica told her.

"You did?"

"You just weren't looking," Monica went on. "Too bad you have to leave. There's nothing like a stroll through the grounds wrapped up in a nice warm cardigan."

"I had this favorite old cardigan once." Susana put down her coffee cup. "It used to be my dad's. It was cream colored and went all the way down to here." She pointed to just below her knees. "And it had this big collar I turned up. I wore it all through high school until it fell apart."

Andrew appeared on the veranda then. "Ladies, good morning," he said, "and happy Thanksgiving."

Megan looked around, wondering where he'd come from. There were no steps behind him.

"Hey, I've got a job for you." Tess took Andrew by the arm and led him to the edge of the porch. "You see that turkey over there?"

"Alexander?"

THE ANGEL OF DEATH (CHARLES ROCKET)
IS RELUCTANT TO KILL THE TURKEY

"What did I tell you?" Tess scolded. "Don't go gettin' sentimental. That's Thanksgiving dinner walking away right there."

Andrew stared at her, starting to get it. "No . . ."

"Dispatch him and make it quick," Tess ordered.

"Come on, Tess, not me—"

"Excuse me," Susana interrupted. "I was hoping Andrew could give me a ride to the service station."

Andrew, Monica, and Tess stared at her.

"Andrew doesn't have a car," Tess said.

"I . . . a friend dropped me off," he explained. "But you know, I do have some experience with things that cease to function. Maybe I can take a look at your cars."

"Go ahead and work on Susana's first," Megan said. It was only fair. Susana had somebody waiting for her. She walked back into the house, and Susana and Tess followed her up the stairs.

"You know, it's going to take Andrew all day to get that car in running order," Megan heard Tess tell Susana as she continued slowly down the hall. "You can fidget around on one foot and get your bloomers in a knot, or you can put on those clothes in your closet and make a day of it. But one way or another, it's going take the same amount of time. Dinner's at eight."

Later that morning Megan walked through the house on her way out to the garden. She was fascinated by the historic contents of the stately mansion: Victorian novels, old games, painted vases, garden statuary, and souvenir monkeys in every size. A small box on a bookshelf caught her eye, and she stopped to pick up an old, pocket-sized camera in a cracked leather case.

Megan noticed an unopened box of film on the shelf, and expertly wove the spool through the casing, snapped it closed, and listened as the shutter clicked. She focused the camera at various objects around the sun-filled room, finally stopping when she saw an antique game highlighted by a shaft of sunlight. She focused carefully and clicked.

"You figure out how to use that old thing?" Tess asked from the doorway where she stood watching her.

"I hope you don't mind," she said, realizing she should have asked before loading the camera. "I'm a photographer. I've always wanted to see what I could get with one of these."

"Could you use a darkroom?" Tess asked.

"I'd love one."

A darkroom? In a house like this? Megan welcomed the opportunity to finish the roll of film and develop the prints.

"I believe there might be one upstairs," Tess told her. "You're welcome to it." She paused. "I've always wanted some pictures of those games. 'Course most people would rather play them—"

Megan smiled. "You play the game and it's over. A picture is forever."

Tess nodded. "Funny thing about a camera. Captures the moment. Funny thing about the moment. There's always a new one." Then she turned and disappeared into the kitchen.

Megan sighed and walked out the back door. Once in the garden, she noticed a small pond with two swans swimming side by side. Nearby stood a gazebo. She climbed the stairs and sat down on a chaise lounge and watched the swans as they circled the pond. She thought of Jack. What was he doing today? Thanksgiving . . .

It was only a moment or two before Monica found her. "What are you thinking?" Monica asked as she sat down on a chair beside Megan.

"Oh, just something I learned in school. Swans. They mate for life."

"'Course the big question is, how long do they live?" Monica said lightly.

Megan tried to smile but couldn't. "This place is so beautiful it's making me depressed."

"I don't understand," Monica said kindly.

"Love. You want to share a place like this with someone you love."

A dove landed on a nearby rock. Monica reached out and stroked its feathers, and the bird flew away.

"Maybe you need to find the beauty in being alone," Monica suggested.

Megan was still pondering Monica's statement long after Monica had left. What had she meant? What could be beautiful about being alone?

She heard footsteps and looked across the pond to see Susana standing on the other side fiddling with her cell phone. She wore a cream-colored cardigan just like she'd described her father wearing. Weird. Really weird. Susana searched the yard with the antenna on her phone, using it like a divining rod, letting it lead the way to water.

And that's what she found. Megan stifled a giggle as she watched Susana cross a narrow footbridge and trip right before she got to the other side.

The cell phone flew high into the air and hit a decorative rock in the shallow water below the bridge. Susana regained her footing and stepped carefully down onto a rock. One foot at a time, she attempted to navigate the pond and retrieve her beloved phone. When she misjudged the distance between her two feet, she lost her balance, tipped, and landed with a huge splash, smack-dab on her behind.

"No! No!" she groaned, slapping the water with her hand. Then, and Megan could hardly believe it, Susana began to laugh. She splashed childishly in the water, laughing hysterically, then waved to an observing duck, and leaned her head back to let the water drench her hair.

"What are you looking at?" Susana asked the llama, who watched from a few feet away. "Haven't you ever made angels in the mud before?" She lifted her arms over her head and brought them down hard into the water, then threw her head back and let the sun hit her face.

Megan watched through the lens of the antique camera. She shot several pictures of a very different person from the one she had met the day before—someone more relaxed. Someone who knew how to enjoy life.

Then she pulled her ankle-length skirt up between her knees and tied it securely. She slipped off her socks and loafers and wandered on out to the edge of the pond near where Susana still lounged. Megan held the camera up and focused it for a close-up shot of Susana, who looked over and smiled.

"Hold really still," Megan told her.

Susana posed playfully for the camera. "Can I get some copies for the *Trial Lawyers Monthly*?" she asked.

"Hold it!" Megan ordered and snapped a picture.

Susana smiled again for the camera, posing with her left side facing Megan and then her right.

"I think I've finally lost it." She shook her head.

"Sanity is overrated," Megan said.

"This is the last place on earth I thought I'd be on Thanksgiving. In a lake in a wet T-shirt contest with a llama."

"What happened?" Megan asked. "Did you get lost yesterday?"

"I didn't think I was lost," Susana answered. "But I guess I took a wrong turn somewhere."

"That's the story of my life." Megan sighed. "You ever wonder how that works? You take a left instead of a right, you cross the street here instead of there, and in one second you've changed your life and you don't even know it?"

Susana nodded. "I met my husband on a street corner. At a newsstand. I wonder where I'd be today if I hadn't stopped for a paper."

"He must be pretty worried about you," Megan said, feeling genuine compassion and just a little envy. At least Susana had someone to worry about her.

Susana looked down into the water, and a shadow fell over her face. "He never worries about me."

"Well, he ought to see you now!" Megan said, laughing.

"I am a mess, aren't I?" Susana said, laughing along with Megan.

"Actually, you look very . . ." Megan searched for the right word. "Elemental, I think. Very natural and very pretty."

Susana shook her head and gave Megan a doubtful look.

"Really," Megan insisted. "Trust me. I make my living doing this. You've got a fabulous profile and this really natural quality that you should let out more."

"That's what my husband always says," Susana said almost bitterly. "I've got a 'great quality.' What about you?" she asked abruptly. "Husband? Boyfriend? Significant other?"

"Significant nightmare," Megan replied, deciding to be honest and trust her new friend.

"Ah," Susana said, nodding. "That's why you're free for Thanksgiving?"

"I always used to laugh at married people who talked about their 'other half.'" Megan snapped a picture of the swans floating together nearby. "Now I know what that means."

"If you find it, hold on to it," Susana advised, "or it slips away."

"I'm trying to, but he's . . . well, it's complicated." How could she ever explain Jack to this married woman so different from herself?

"It's always complicated," Susana said thoughtfully. "But sometimes it's worth it."

A few hours later, Megan followed Monica up a back staircase that led into an immense attic. The two women wandered through dusty boxes and trunks and into a corner where a makeshift darkroom was set up.

"I hope this is what you need," Monica said.

"This is great." Megan surveyed the equipment—the brown bottles of chemicals, contact paper, trays, a line for drying the photographs—it was all here. Megan was sure she could develop her pictures.

"If you want to grab the light . . ." Megan said.

Monica hit the light switch and the darkness engulfed them.

"You're pretty good at it, aren't you?" Monica said as she peered over Megan's shoulder. "Picture taking?"

"Some people think so."

"Why do you suppose people take pictures?" Monica asked.

Megan pondered that for a moment. "I think, deep down, it's our way of declaring war on death. You take a picture of something, and even if it goes away, you'll still have a piece of it."

Monica didn't respond right away. "Seems to me it's better to have all of it for a while than a piece of it forever."

Megan smiled to herself as she gripped the corner of the photo sheet and laid it gently in a tray of developing solution.

"We need to let it sit here for just a second or two," Megan told Monica, who was still looking on. "Wait till you see this. I think I got off some great shots. Susana's so pretty, and she doesn't even know it."

A head and shoulders shot of Susana sitting up in the pond slowly began to reveal itself to Megan and Monica. Megan removed it from the solution and fastened it with a tiny clip to a string to dry. As she had predicted, the woman looked radiant, sensual, and completely at ease.

"Wait till she sees this," Megan said proudly and hurried from the room to look for Susana. She stopped abruptly on the landing, though, when she saw Tess holding the front door open for a man—Jack! What was he doing here? What was going on?

"She was supposed to meet me last night out near the lake," he was telling Tess as he entered the hallway. "But she never showed up. I figured she got caught up in some business thing, but . . ."

Megan watched as Susana came from the parlor into the hallway. She was wearing a woven white pants outfit. Her hair fell softly around her shoulders.

"Sunny?" Jack was obviously startled by her appearance. Megan couldn't believe this. What was happening?

"Jack!" Susana exclaimed in delight.

What? They knew each other?

They hugged, and Jack stepped away to look at Susana in full view.

"Are you all right?" he asked.

"I had an accident," Susana said softly. "A little one. I'm fine, but there's no phone."

"Thank God." Jack sighed and pulled Susana close to him. "I thought I'd lost you."

Susana was Jack's wife! Megan tried desperately to back away, but Monica was standing right behind her. Before either of them could move, Susana looked up from Jack's shoulder and spotted them.

"Monica! Megan!" she cried. "Come down here. I want you to meet my husband, Jack."

Jack looked up, and his happy face went pale. His mouth fell open as Megan walked numbly down the flight of stairs and extended her hand.

"Hello," Megan said, unable to look him in the eyes. She focused on the top button of his suede jacket. "I . . . just met . . . your wife yesterday. It was an accident."

"Ah, well . . ." Jack couldn't seem to talk at all.

"It wasn't a big accident," Monica said. "Nobody was hurt, but the car isn't going anywhere right now. By the way, I'm Monica."

Jack nodded at the women, as he held tightly onto Susana's arm. "They let us stay here overnight," Susana said. "How did you find me?"

"Well, uh, when you didn't show up and you didn't answer at home, I called everywhere I could think of, and then I just got in the car and started looking."

"You really were worried, weren't you?" Susana said in a swooning kind of tone as she reached up to pull Jack's face down so she could kiss him on the cheek.

Megan couldn't remember ever feeling so much pain in her life.

"Well, here you are," Jack said nervously, "and you're fine. Let's get your stuff and go. We'll come back for the car later."

"Oh, but I promised to stay for Thanksgiving dinner," Susana told him. "This is such a wonderful place and I'm just starting to relax." Susana turned to Tess. "Do you . . . still want us . . ."

"Oh, the more the merrier," Tess exclaimed as she sized Jack up. "What are you, Jack, about a forty-four long?"

"Uh . . . yeah . . ."

Megan was speechless. She crumpled the photograph of Susana she held behind her back, but even that offered her no relief from the incredible hurt she was feeling.

"Well, we'd better get started then," Monica said behind her. "I could really use some help in the kitchen, Megan."

Megan turned to give Monica a grateful glance and then followed her to the kitchen. Away from Jack. Away from the pain that held her in a death grip as long she stood there.

In the kitchen, Monica handed Megan a large wicker basket, and the two of them went out into the garden to select fresh vegetables for dinner. They worked quietly for several minutes, filling the basket with beans, corn, peppers, carrots, squash, and sweet potatoes.

"I was thinking I'd make a pumpkin pie," Monica broke the silence. "Unless you know how to. I've never made one, but it is either that or let Tess make mincemeat. Let's see—it's you, me, Tess, Andrew, Susana, and Jack. Do you think four squash will be enough?"

"Jack doesn't like squash," Megan said without thinking. She gasped as she realized what she had said to Monica. Stopping, she covered her face with her hands, trying to hold back the tears.

"This must be so difficult for you, Megan," Monica said.

Megan stared at Monica. How did she know? What did she know?

"I saw the picture of Jack in your room," Monica explained.

"Does it show?" Megan asked anxiously. "Do you think she knows?"

Monica shook her head.

Megan sat back in the grass and crossed her legs up under her skirt. "You know," she began, "she was never real before today. There was this weekend a few months ago when Jack was able to get away 'on business.' We were driving through the lake country to a bed-and-breakfast we'd heard about. We took a shortcut through the woods and all of a sudden, it was like some deep forest on the other side of the world. The road was so narrow we could barely get through, and the trees were so thick we couldn't see the sky. And it was quiet. It was so quiet. We were totally alone and totally happy together. I could have died right then and there." She looked up at Monica, who seemed engrossed in what she was saying. "And then all of a sudden his car phone rang. I didn't say anything. And he didn't say anything. It rang and it rang and we both knew it was 'her.' It kept ringing, and then we started talking, casually, over the ringing, trying to pretend it wasn't happening. But there we were, in the middle of nowhere, and she was there with us, begging to be heard. And we just ignored her, like somebody trapped in the trunk, screaming to be let out. And when the ringing finally stopped, we never talked about it. And that's who I thought she was. A distant bell that you hear, but just ignore. She wasn't real until now." Megan's voice broke, and she couldn't hold back the tears. "What should I do? I can't leave and I can't stay," she sobbed.

"This is what you call an unexpected snow," Monica said, reaching over to pat her arm.

An unexpected snow? What was Monica talking about?

"An unexpected snow," Monica repeated. "One moment the sky looks clear, and the next moment, the sky is falling. You can run inside and hide, or you can become part of it and let it change you."

Megan stared at her. Something was ringing true, but she couldn't quite put her finger on it.

Later that day Monica, Tess, and Andrew sat on the back steps looking at Alexander the turkey, who stood a few feet away and almost seemed to smile back at them.

"You said you wanted to help out around here, Angel Boy," Tess reminded a reluctant Andrew.

"But this is like inviting your accountant over for dinner and asking him to balance your checkbook," Andrew said morosely.

"You beat all, you know that," Tess said in a disgusted tone. "Would you just please do it?"

"But look at that face." Andrew pointed to the turkey. "Behold, the noble turkey. Did you know that Ben Franklin actually proposed the turkey as the national bird?"

Tess waved a hand. "Ben Franklin was a nosy little motormouth who never had sense enough to come in out of the rain. Now I want that turkey on the table at eight!"

Andrew heaved a great sigh and looked at Monica. She shrugged and followed Tess into the house.

A grandfather clock struck eight o'clock, and the guests filed into the dining room for a traditional holiday feast. Tess, Monica, and Megan had outdone themselves. A roasted turkey sat on a platter in the middle of the table, garnished with fresh and colorful vegetables and fruits from the estate gardens. Stuffing, mashed potatoes, and cranberry sauce filled cut crystal bowls. The best china, sterling, and glassware were arranged perfectly on an antique lace tablecloth. The chandelier was dimmed, and the room glowed with candlelight.

The guests were festively dressed in clothes left by their hosts. Susana, in particular, was radiant in an off-the-shoulder dress and knotted shawl.

Megan edged into her chair, looking at everyone and everything but Jack. Andrew took Susana's right hand, and she extended her left to Jack. He hesitated a moment, then awkwardly took Megan's hand with his left, and when the circle was finally complete, Monica asked everyone to bow their heads.

"Thank You, Lord," she began, "for this Thanksgiving meal, and thank You for the hands that prepared it. Thank You for all the gifts we take for granted every day, like pumpkins and llamas and stars and snow. Thank You for always remembering the big things, like oxygen and the sun com-

A THANKSGIVING DINNER IN "AN UNEXPECTED SNOW"
(L TO R: NANCY ALLEN, ROMA, DELLA, CHARLES
ROCKET, BROOKE ADAMS, ED MARINARO)

ing up every day, and the little things, like cranberry sauce and fiber optics." She paused. "Thank You especially for bringing us all here together today."

Megan opened her eyes to peek at Jack. He had his head bowed, but his eyes were open. He must have sensed her watching, for he immediately looked up, and their eyes locked for the first time since he'd arrived.

"It may not be the Thanksgiving everybody had planned," Monica went on, "but I guess it was the one You had planned, so bless the hearts around this table, amen."

Andrew stood to carve the turkey, and everyone began to talk and pass their plates to him. Megan and Jack were subdued in comparison to the others. Megan couldn't remember when she'd ever landed in a more awkward and painful situation—one where she had to try to act as normal as possible.

"What's in this dressing?" Andrew asked, taking a huge bite.

"That's an old recipe I picked up a few years back," Tess said.

"That squash looks wonderful," Susana said. "I'll take Jack's share—he doesn't like it."

"Please pass the cranberries . . ."

Megan stared at the food on her plate and realized she'd lost her appetite.

"Oh, I forgot the gravy," Tess said, starting to get up.

Megan quickly leapt to her feet, motioning for Tess to sit back down. "Let me get it for you," she said and rushed off to the kitchen.

Megan could hear the muted conversation from where she stood at the sink looking out over the garden and trying to choke down the sobs that kept struggling for expression. Then she heard Jack's voice.

"You know what I could use?" he was saying. "Another napkin. I can see I'm going to need another one." A pause. "Anybody want napkins? I'm already up!" And then he was backing into the kitchen.

Megan moved quickly to the range where she busied herself pouring the thick brown sauce into a china gravy boat.

"How—how did this happen?" he hissed as he came up beside her at the stove.

"I swear I didn't know who she was until you walked in the door," she said, waving the gravy ladle in his face. "Why didn't you tell me Sunny's name was Susana?"

"What were you doing on this road anyway? I told you to take the interstate back."

"You told me she was the ice queen," Megan whispered, near tears again. "She's wonderful. She's sweet. You don't give her enough credit."

"This is my worst nightmare," Jack said as he leaned on the counter and dropped his chin into his right hand, then just shook his head in despair.

"How do you think I feel?" Megan asked. "The only thing worse than spending holidays away from you is spending them with you *and* your wife!"

"You just said you liked her!"

"I do like her, that's the problem. You've got great taste in women!"

"This is crazy." Jack rubbed a hand through his graying hair and paced across the kitchen. "Look, let's just get through this and ... and I'll work something out."

"You've been saying that for over a year now."

"I know. It's just taking longer than I thought it would."

"Well, maybe there's a reason for that," Megan said slowly. She knew this was not the perfect time or place to address it, but was there ever a perfect time or place to do the right thing? "I love you, Jack, I really do. But I always thought you were miserable with her and that I was the one who would make you happy."

"You are. You do," he assured her.

"I knew you had a wife," she said, her eyes penetrating his, "I just didn't realize you were married." She picked up the gravy boat and left Jack standing in the kitchen.

The kitchen sink was piled high with the aftermath of Thanksgiving dinner: the sticky residue of sweet potatoes on a casserole dish, gravy coagulated around the base of the boat, the turkey carcass, cranberry stains on every plate.

"Do you think there's really any virtue in washing dishes?" Tess asked as she stood glaring at the dishes.

Monica shrugged. "I think it builds character."

"I've got enough character. I want some pie."

Tess turned her back to the sink and began to cut into the pumpkin pies that waited on the butcher-block table. She sliced each into six pieces and turned back to the sink to clean the knife. It was empty of dishes, and the counter was spotless. Monica smiled. Ordinary miracles were sometimes necessary when other, more important things were going on—like people's lives hanging in the balance in the next room.

"This could still go either way, you know," Tess said.

"How can love cause so much pain?" Monica asked.

"When there's that much pain, you gotta ask yourself if it's really love," Tess said wisely. "People hold on to each other for lots of reasons they don't understand, and they call it love. But it's really fear."

"Fear?"

"The girl goes around taking pictures of things so that she can remember what she never had in case she loses it." Tess shook her head. "This affair? It's not love. It's just a picture of the real thing."

"Don't you think somebody should be talking with Jack?" Monica asked.

"Oh, I'll talk to Jack, all right," Tess said, nodding. "He's responsible for a great deal of pain here. But your job is to help Megan. One woman's destiny can have a way of overlapping onto other people's lives." She handed Monica two plates to take to their guests. "Everybody can leave this house on a new path. But only if Megan finds the courage to take the first step."

A short time later everyone moved into the parlor where Monica and Tess passed out pieces of pie. Megan sat staring into the roaring fire across from Susana and Jack, who sat close together on the tapestry sofa examining the antique game on the coffee table. Susana rotated the cage, then opened the tiny gate, withdrew a ball, and read the question.

"If you had to spend the rest of your life on a desert island, who would you want with you?" Susana read from the paper.

"A boat builder," Andrew called from the corner.

"Who would you choose, Jack?" Susana poked her husband.

He stared at her, and as she looked down to the paper again, Monica watched Jack and Megan exchange a quick glance.

"It's okay. It doesn't have to be me." Susana smiled. "You'd probably choose somebody who plays poker."

"You play poker?" Megan asked, apparently not knowing her lover as well as she thought she did.

Jack smiled weakly, and Susana gave the cage a second spin.

"What is it about this place?" Susana said, shaking her head. "I'm playing dumb games, and I haven't thought about work for an entire day. I even drowned my cell phone. I think Megan has had a good influence on me." She pulled another piece of paper out of the cage and read it aloud. "Describe your happiest day and why you remember it. That's a nice Thanksgiving question . . ."

This game was just too painful for some of them in the room, Monica decided. "Why don't you sing something, Tess?" she suggested, then turned to the group. "She has a lovely voice."

Tess took any and every opportunity to showcase her voice. So, with Andrew on the keyboard, she began a blues rendition of "What Is This Thing Called Love?"

Monica watched as Susana and Jack talked in hushed tones and then finally rose from the sofa to go upstairs to bed. On the landing, with Susana a few steps ahead of him, he turned back around to look at Megan where she sat near the fireplace. Megan's face was full of agony as she turned away and stared into the dying fire.

Later that night Megan lay on her bed for a long time staring up at the ceiling. She wished she could cry—maybe

TESS ENTERTAINS A CAPTIVE AUDIENCE

it would help—but she just felt . . . numb. Finally she decided to take a walk in the garden. She wrapped her robe around herself and crept downstairs and out of the house onto the terrace. Then she walked slowly through the garden, finally stopping at the pond where she reached down to pick up a pebble. She hurled it fiercely into the water, then picked up another one and threw it a little harder. And another. Finally she was throwing rocks and the tears started and wouldn't stop. She crumpled to her knees, sobbing.

Jack . . . it was coming to an end . . . *they* were coming to an end. She'd known it would probably happen, but she'd hoped he might leave his wife, yet she knew he wouldn't . . .

She heard a rustling in the grass and looked up to see Monica walking toward her.

"Do you know what the name 'Megan' means?" Monica asked as she stopped beside Megan.

Megan shook her head.

"A pearl of great value. Something very precious that deserves to be cherished, not wasted."

"All this time I told myself we . . . we had something special." Megan's shoulders finally stopped shaking as she tried to talk. "But tonight when he looked over his shoulder at me and walked up the stairs with her, I realized, 'My God, I'm just the "other woman."' He's been keeping me in a room I didn't even know I was in. And tonight he's left me alone in there."

"You walked into that room all by yourself," Monica said gently.

Megan nodded. It was the truth. "I did the one thing I swore I'd never do. It's just that . . . well, after awhile you spend enough nights alone and you go to too many other people's weddings and baby showers. You spend too many holidays at other people's houses, and you just want a little piece of their happiness for yourself, you know. Just for a while. Just so you can say someday that somebody wanted you, that somebody thought you were worth it."

She broke down again, and she felt Monica's arm go around her shoulder.

Monica cleared her throat. "Megan, wanting to love someone and wanting to be loved in return, those things are good and right. But wanting them from someone else's husband is wrong."

"He's not supposed to be married," Megan argued. "He's supposed to be with me. God made a mistake."

"If something gets this ugly and this painful, God had nothing to do with it," Monica explained.

"Then I wish He'd tell me what to do now."

Monica smiled. "He's just about to."

A gentle snow began to fall, and Megan turned her face up to the sky to feel the flakes.

"When you cry, God cries too, Megan. But He can only dry your tears if you let Him."

Megan's head was beginning to clear now. "The road I took the other day . . . it wasn't an accident, was it?"

Monica shook her head.

"And this place?"

"This house was created for you. For this night. For this moment. The unexpected snow."

Megan got to her feet and stood looking at Monica with wonder, but then she pictured Jack's loving face close to hers . . .

"Well, I can't . . . ," she cried, "I can't let him go. I won't. You can tell God that. Why can't He just let me have this one thing I really want?"

MONICA COMFORTS MEGAN (NANCY ALLEN) IN HER SOLITUDE

"Because there's a better love for you, Megan," Monica said knowingly. "We don't know where and we don't know when. But the only love worth having you won't have to lie for, or steal, or keep in a box and visit on weekends."

"Well, it may not be great love," Megan argued, "but it's *my* love."

"No, it isn't, Megan. It belongs to Susana."

Megan stared at Monica. The snow stopped abruptly, and Megan looked around her. What . . . But when she turned back to Monica, she had disappeared.

Megan used clothespins to hang the photographs of Susana on the string to dry. She stepped back to look at them and heard a knock at the door.

"Come in," she said. It was probably Monica come up to watch her work.

"Megan?"

She turned to see Jack standing hesitantly in the doorway.

"I didn't know where you were until Monica mentioned there was a darkroom."

They stood quietly for a moment, and then Jack noticed the photos of Susana hanging above them.

"She really is beautiful, isn't she?" Megan said.

"She's got a great quality about her."

"No, she's beautiful," Megan corrected him. "*And* she's got a great quality about her." She paused. "Can I ask you a question?" She didn't wait for him to answer. "If you had to spend the rest of your life on a desert island, who would you want to spend it with?"

Jack seemed embarrassed and refused to meet her eyes.

"That's what I thought," Megan said. "And guess what, you *are* on a desert island." She pulled the driest photographs down from the string. "You know, you're not a bad guy. You're a bad husband. If you put half as much energy into being a good husband as you put into being a good lover, you could have a great marriage." She handed him the photos. "I don't know if that's what you want, but that's what I want for you. And that's what I want for myself."

Jack studied the photos he held in his hand. "You know, that woman, Tess, talked to me today. She said something like, 'When two people are on a journey, there will be miles when they'll fall silent, but that doesn't mean they shouldn't be traveling together.'" He grunted. "It makes sense." He looked at her then. "But I love you, too, Megan."

She nodded. "I know. As much as you can. But we both know it's not right. And the harder we try to make it seem right, it just bends more and more out of shape until it doesn't even feel like love anymore. I want to stop before we turn it into something else completely."

He stared at her. "How can . . . how do I let go of you . . ."

Megan hesitated. "I'm already gone." And she turned away.

The front yard bustled with activity as everyone prepared to leave. Monica motioned to Megan to follow her away from the group and over to the side of the yard.

"There are going to be some lonely nights ahead, Megan," Monica began. "And when those times come, just remember . . ." She brought a child's snow globe from behind her back. ". . . you may be lonely, but you're never alone." Monica handed the snow globe to Megan.

Megan looked up at her. "Will I ever see you again?"

Monica shook her head. "Probably not any time soon, but I promise you this. I'll dance at your wedding, my girl."

Megan felt a warmth inside at the thought of marriage to a man who would truly be hers, and Monica looking on with beaming joy and approval.

"Thank you," she said, and turned to see Jack helping Susana slip into her cardigan sweater. Megan smiled at Monica, then forced herself to walk back to the group.

Andrew saw her coming and held her car keys out to her. He handed another set to Susana. "The cars are all fixed, gassed, and waiting at the gate," he said proudly.

"I'll give you two a lift," Jack offered.

"You go ahead," Susana said. "I want to say good-bye to Megan."

Megan was surprised at this. She smiled at Susana.

Jack nervously clapped his hands together. "Okay, well . . ." He turned to Megan. "Well, it was nice to meet you." He hesitated. "Take care of yourself." He stuck his hand out, and Megan shook it briefly, knowing it was the last time they would ever touch each other.

"You too," she said.

Jack turned to Susana. "I'll . . . meet you at home?"

She nodded. "I'll be right behind you."

Jack started to get into his car.

"Hey, Jack, how about giving Andrew a lift into town?" Tess asked.

"Uh, sure. You got any bags?"

"No, I guess I don't."

Andrew climbed into the car beside Jack then, and everyone waved as the car rolled down the driveway. Megan and Susana watched it disappear around the first bend in the road. Then they gave a last wave to Tess and Monica and turned to walk down the tree-lined drive.

"Are you driving back to the city?" Susana asked finally, breaking the silence.

"Yeah."

"I had a wonderful time. I'm glad we 'ran into each other.'"

"So am I, Susana," Megan agreed. "I really, really am."

They were nearing the gate when Susana stopped and turned to Megan.

"My husband talks in his sleep. You know what he says?" She hesitated for a moment. "He says, 'Megan.'"

Megan stared at Susana.

"I've had a name for a long time," Susana went on, "but I haven't had a face. I'm sorry it had to be yours."

Megan wanted to say something, but what could she possibly say that would make any difference at this point?

"When I first met you after the accident, it seemed impossible to me that you could be 'that' Megan. But when I saw you and Jack together in the same room, I knew."

"I never meant to hurt anybody," Megan blurted. "I just . . . I'm sorry. I'm so sorry. But believe me, it's over. It really is. Will you forgive me?"

Susana was quiet for a moment, then she sighed. "When I was on my way to meet Jack for the long weekend I knew there was a very strong possibility that this would be our last Thanksgiving. But somehow, I ended up here and for the first time in years, I feel like maybe we've got a chance." She looked at Megan. "I recognized something in you that I've been missing in myself. I guess Jack has missed it, too." She started to walk again. "It might be a little early to talk about forgiveness, but I know it will come."

What else could Megan ask of her?

"These holidays are killers," Tess said as the two angels stood at the top of the driveway watching Megan and Susana climb into their cars and drive off.

"Yeah, and I was wondering, can I keep the llama?" Monica asked with a grin.

"Don't start with me, girl."

They turned to look behind them, and the beautiful chateau was gone. Tess and Monica and the llama stood in an open field.

"Happy Thanksgiving, Tess. I'm very thankful for you, you know."

"Thankful is as thankful does, Miss Wings!"

And with a gust of wind, the angels were gone. ⌒

Response to the Show

Roma Downey

During the filming, we faced a few challenges. For instance, we had trouble keeping the llama in position. And we had to simulate snow using potato flakes. During one scene, a flake stayed on my lip, stubbornly refusing to melt—because, of course, potato flakes don't behave like real snow.

Little did I imagine when we were traipsing through the rooms of the mansion filming the show that I'd be back for my wedding. Della performed the ceremony, marrying David and me in the house where "An Unexpected Snow" was filmed.

Nancy Allen—Megan

My brother died the week before I agreed to be in a *Touched by an Angel* episode. I wanted to do the show because I love the series. . . . People advised against it because I had just lost my brother and needed time to grieve. But I found myself in the evenings knowing I was in exactly the right place. Della is very spiritual, and Roma has experienced a lot of loss. What better place for me to be than with people who had been living in the midst of a show about God and angels?

FROM VIEWERS

The episode that makes me cry as I write is the Thanksgiving show dealing with infidelity. Unfortunately, it hit a bit too close to home—you see, my husband had a "friend." I found out last spring. We're continually working on this marriage. Your program was interesting, realistic, and encouraging. The angel's words still echo, "When things get this bad, God has nothing to do with it." How true! How wonderful life would be if people could realize this truth!

Atlanta, Georgia

I am not married but had a cheating husband, and once I was the "other woman" after my divorce. I know now how I really offended God and the wife. I have heard for years that to love others you have to love and forgive yourself first. Well, I got the whole picture, as Tess said in the program. Our lives are not about how we feel, but about the moments, and we can always start over to do the right thing.

Chicago, Illinois

CHAPTER 5

JACOB'S LADDER

Monica: "Nothing, not death or life or war, not the present, or the future, or the past, no one, no creature on this earth can separate you from the love of God."

The Story Behind the Story

*W*hat if Monica was committed to a mental hospital for thinking she was an angel?

One of the biggest challenges we face on *Touched by an Angel* is how to show presumably "perfect" angels in conflict. The answer is that angels aren't perfect. That's one of the "theological rules" of the series.

Every television series needs a set of rules that the writers can follow to keep the episodes consistent. Usually, it doesn't matter what the rules are, as long as they don't change. Otherwise, the audience gets confused, frustrated, and finally disenchanted.

Star Trek, for example, began with an unlimited galaxy and a single Federation "prime directive." Then, Gene Roddenberry brilliantly populated the universe with Klingons and Vulcans and other fantastic creatures. Their habits and peculiarities were easily accepted because, until then, no one had ever heard of Klingons and Vulcans.

Angels were a whole different ball game. Angels have been depicted in art and written of in Scripture and literature for centuries. Everyone, if they think about angels at all, has a very personal idea of what an angel is, what an angel looks like, and how an angel should act.

On top of that, when you're talking about angels, you're talking about God. And to most people, God means religion, and folks just don't trust television to treat religion with much respect. As a matter of fact, many, many letters our second year were from new converts to the show who had purposely avoided *Touched* the first season because they were afraid of what Hollywood would do to angels.

People who believe in angels don't like to see them trivialized or expanded into wish-granting fairies. On the other hand, angel enthusiasts vary greatly in their beliefs and experience. It was inevitable that we were not going to please all the people all the time.

Nevertheless, we had to start somewhere when we were hired to redesign the series. With only three weeks to create a "show bible," the natural place to turn was to the Bible itself. There, it was clear that angels had very specific duties and purposes: to deliver messages, to comfort, to protect, and occasionally to deliver healing.

Some of the other "Touched by an Angel" rules we follow are:

a. Angels do not have power over life and death. That's what God is for. Besides, if Monica raised somebody from the dead one week, what could she possibly do for an encore?

b. Angels do not lie. "Love is our job and truth is our stock in trade," says Sam, the "secret angel" played by Emmy-award-winning actor Paul Winfield. In one episode, Monica evades the truth, tells a lie by omission, and is banished to an unidentified netherworld. It is the same place Tess visited when she confronted Satan with hate instead of love.

c. Angels do not disobey God's orders without serious consequences. God doesn't make mistakes, even if the plan is not clear to humans or angels. He knows what He's doing; He's been doing this for years!

d. Angels, in the strictest of terms, do not "have faith." "Faith is the substance of things unseen," Monica reminds us. And having seen God and His kingdom, angels already know what we humans must simply have faith in. It is that quality of faith and the occasional doubts we must overcome that give humans a strength that angels can only admire.

e. Angels are not superstitious. "Luck," says Tess, "is when God wishes to remain anonymous."

f. Angels cannot change the past, nor do they predict or see into the future. Only in rare cases are they given revelation from God which, in turn, they are bound to reveal to a human. When a teenage unwed mother struggles to give up her baby for adoption ("Cassie's Choice"), Monica is allowed to reassure the girl that her daughter has inherited her musical talent and will become a great musician.

g. Angels do not allow themselves to be the focus of worship. Their purpose is to serve and glorify their Creator.

h. Angels must perform their duties on earth with human bodies that don't always do what they want them to do. Their bodies, though perfectly healthy, are often susceptible to human frailty and temptation. One of Monica's most charming "flaws" is her weakness for coffee, especially decaf mocha latte. Because her body has been relatively unsullied by earthbound life, she and other angels will occasionally have negative and even dangerous responses to toxins, drugs, and new experiences. One of the best examples occurs in the following episode of "Jacob's Ladder," where an unusual reaction to medication allowed us to showcase more of Roma Downey's exceptional acting range.

i. Special dispensation—occasionally, God will lift the rules of nature or time or physics to accomplish His purpose. The dying father in "Till We Meet Again" stunned his family by leaving his deathbed to serenade them one last time on the family piano. Events like this fall under the Big Miracle Category.

j. The Angel of Death is nothing to be afraid of. He does not pick the day or the hour of death. Nor does he dispense judgment. Being the Angel of Death is a plum job for any angel, a privilege and a sacred responsibility.

There have been three angels of death since *Touched* premiered. The loopy and endearing Charles Rocket is best remembered for stubbornly saving the life of Tess's Thanksgiving turkey. The charming and philosophical Bruce Altman joined us the second season and lent a certain debonair inevitability to his last rites.

Finally, John Dye joined us, playing an angel of death who was a former caseworker and protégé of Tess's. John, a gentleman from Mississippi, brought great love and energy to this role. We loved him so much that we were tempted to start killing off all the characters just so we could have him back every week. Finally, we asked him to join the series as a regular, and the duties of the Angel of Death have now been expanded to utilize Andrew's casework experience.

k. Angels are not all in the choir. Somewhat tone-deaf Monica, for example, didn't perform well there, and was quickly transferred to other "departments"— Annunciations, Search and Rescue, Casework, etc.

One angel, however, sings like no other. Della Reese has a star on Hollywood Boulevard that commemorates not only her television and film career, but her incredible life as a musician and singer. Having Della on the show and not taking advantage of that voice would be like keeping Charles Barkley on the bench during the play-offs. So, we always keep a lookout for a Della Reese solo. One of the happiest days we had on the set was Della's "Indigo Angel" jam session with B. B. King, Al Jarreau, Dr. John, Al Hirt, and Hal Linden sitting in on clarinet. "Died and gone to heaven" was the phrase most often heard that afternoon. The least popular guy in town was director, Jon Andersen, who finally had to yell, "Cut!"

l. Angels, though capable of performing small miracles with the power God allows them, prefer to rely on truth rather than tricks to make a point. Occasionally, as happens in the following story, Monica will find herself without any power at all, except her gift of sharing God's love with words. Such circumstances inevitably teach Monica another lesson in faith and in the human condition.

m. Angels work on a "need to know" basis. They don't know everything. God does. Sometimes Tess and Monica begin an assignment without all the details. Occasionally, Tess cannot reveal the whole plan to Monica or Andrew. Then they just have to "wing it."

n. Angels are not "recycled dead people," but created beings, creatures fashioned by God. They are not and never were human, but they possess the very human gift of free will. It allows them, as it does us, to make our own choices. Usually, angels make the right ones. Fortunately, sometimes the plot thickens when they make the wrong choices. Thank God for free will. We couldn't write television shows without it!

God's gift of free will has provided Monica with her most interesting choices, and occasionally her worst mistakes. And yet, she is still an angel. As representatives of heaven, Monica, Tess, and Andrew must all maintain a divine and loving nature.

Roma Downey, Della Reese, and John Dye have three of the hardest jobs in television. How do you play a completely loving, hardly flawed character week after week and keep yourself interesting? First of all, you believe in what you are doing. The passionate faith of Della, the complete sincerity of Roma, and John's strong personal beliefs turn some of TV's most difficult dialogue into powerful truth. The stars' genuine commitment to their roles is matched only by their genuine talent. It takes great skill to make angels our accessible friends and yet unearthly creatures.

"Jacob's Ladder" explores that mysterious realm between heaven and earth where angels spend so much time. It is a unique episode in that it seems to break practically every one of our "angel rules." What happens to angels who fail? What happens when angels forget the very message they have been sent to share? What happens when angels forget God Himself and begin to display the human qualities of guilt, self-doubt, and fear?

And yet, just when we've written ourselves into a tight theological corner, we discover once again that God is faithful. As Monica reassures her fallen friend: "Nothing . . . can separate us from the love of God."

And that is the best "angel rule" of all.

—M. W.

JACOB'S LADDER

TELEPLAY BY MARTHA WILLIAMSON
STORY BY KEN LAZEBNIK

If an angel called Monica had ever needed, or wanted, a last name, it would certainly not have been "Doe." But when caught "holding the bag," this angel found herself at the wrong place at the right time and thus became Ms. Monica Doe.

*M*onica watched the disheveled man as he slept on an old mattress next to what looked like a pile of dirty laundry. A blanket was bunched up at the end of the mattress, and a trail of clothing led down a hallway. Towels hung over the back of every chair, several tall plastic cups sat on each arm of the sofa, and four empty green bottles stood side by side on a bedside table. The tenant looked to be about twenty-five years old, and it was obvious that he cared little about the condition of his home. Clothes, magazines, CDs, and four stereo speakers, their wires dangling, were scattered about the floor. An open carton of stale chocolate donuts sat on a shelf by the television set, and a bag of cheese puffs was spilled out over the broken recliner.

The house was atypical of the domestic settings that Monica had visited most often. The angel watched curiously as the man's snores steadily escalated in volume. Her next assignment was supposed to be a kindergarten teacher. Could it be—those poor five-year-olds? This man needed a maid more than he needed an angel.

"What are you doing *here*, baby?" Tess's resounding voice interrupted Monica's thoughts. Almost accusatory, somewhat maternal, all supervisorial. The appearance of her mentor was a tremendous relief.

Monica looked down at the address she'd written on her palm in ballpoint ink. She was in the right place.

"It's right here," she said. "801 Cedar Street, Jacksonville. Terry Hayman. He sure doesn't look like a schoolteacher, though, does he?"

The man rolled over, exposing his naked belly, and snorted as he scrunched up into a comfortable position once again.

"For heaven's sake," Tess exclaimed. "It's Jacksonville, Illinois, not Jacksonville, Florida! Am I my angel's keeper? Let's get outta here, girl. Terry Hayman is standing in her bedroom at this very moment, packing her bags. And you gotta get there before she leaves her husband and runs away with his accountant."

Monica was sure she'd been dispatched to Florida and, if anyone needed an angel, it was this pathetic man. Tess was already halfway down the front steps, but Monica couldn't resist the temptation to work a minor miracle first. Always leave a room neater than the way you found it, or so she was taught in training.

And so for the next few minutes, she busied herself restacking the CDs on the coffee table, hanging the towels in the bathroom, tossing the bottles in the recycling bin, washing and folding the laundry, and arranging fresh flowers in a vase by the bed.

"Every day is a new opportunity to start over," she told the man in the bed. Maybe waking up to a clean house would lead him to think twice about his lifestyle.

As Monica surveyed her handiwork one last time, she noticed something unusual sticking out from underneath the mattress. Careful not to disturb the man, she bent over to pick up the lumpy brown paper bag.

Without warning, the lights in the house flashed on, and six police officers in helmets and bulletproof vests burst through the doorway.

"Police! Freeze! Do not move or we will shoot! We will shoot!"

The man jumped off his mattress and ran to the open window. One of the officers fired a shot into the ceiling, and Monica jumped three feet into the air. The man simply threw his hands up over his head. Had he been through this drill before?

"Drop it, hands up!" a burly SWAT officer screamed at her.

"I'm sorry," she began, dropping the bag and shaking in terror. "If I'd known it was an important bag—"

"Shut up!" he yelled. "And keep your hands above your head!"

One officer handcuffed the man who was now very wide awake, while another officer picked up the bag at Monica's feet. He pulled out a plastic sack of white powder, dusted a finger with the substance, and touched it to his tongue. He nodded to his partner, then the officer roughly clamped a pair of handcuffs around Monica's wrists.

Was this really happening? Monica had never done anything wrong in her entire life, and that was a very long time to be good. Where was Tess?

"Okay, lady," the officer began. "You are under arrest. You have the right to remain silent. Anything you say can and will be used against you in a court of law. You have the right to have an attorney present during questioning. If you cannot afford an attorney, one will be appointed for you . . ."

What a ridiculous mess. She could never clear this up by herself. Where in the world was Tess?

Monica sat at a formica-topped table, now bubbling and cracked from years of fist pounding and overall wear. Many a creative suspect had scratched a name or ugly reference in the finish. She was eager to clear up the misunderstanding that had landed her here at police headquarters in the middle of the night and be on her way. She frowned at the tape recorder in front of her.

"No driver's license?" The arresting officer, Frank Cates, eyed her suspiciously.

"Well, I don't drive." Monica tried to smooth out the wrinkles in her simple flowered dress and white crocheted sweater. "Well, sometimes I drive the Cadillac, but Tess doesn't like it. She's never actually come right out and said it, but I can tell. You work with somebody that long and—"

"This Tess is your partner?" Cates questioned.

"I guess you could call her my supervisor. You see, I'm—"

"Supervisor?" Cates's eyes narrowed and he sat back in his chair. "Sounds like you've got quite an organization going."

"Oh, yes," Monica agreed. "In our business, you have to be organized."

The officer looked pleased, and Monica was glad she could be of so much help.

She chuckled. "Of course, I wasn't too organized tonight."

"Were you delivering or picking up?" Cates asked.

Monica looked at him, confused. "Picking up?"

"Picking up for Tess or dropping off?"

"Uh, well, I was just meeting her there. Well, not there, actually. I was supposed to meet her at 801 Cedar Street, but in Jacksonville, Illinois, not Florida." She showed him the numbers still written on her palm.

The second officer in the room immediately reached behind him to a shelf where he grabbed a camera and snapped a shot of her hand.

"I wrote it down, but I forgot to put the state," Monica went on. "It's always so confusing. States, countries, borders. Such a human thing!" She waved a hand at him. "I suppose I should pay more attention, but it's hard to take borders seriously in my work."

"That's the problem with you people," Cates said with disgust. "No ID, no known address, no yellow sheet, no fingerprints on file, no nothing. How long have you and Tess been operating your little drug ring?"

Monica stared at him in shock. "Excuse me?"

Cates gestured to his partner. "Munson and I know every dope dealer in this state. How come we never heard of you?"

"You—you think I'm a drug person?"

Cates shrugged. "Call me crazy. Maybe it was the two kilos you were holding when we met."

Monica's stomach began to knot. Maybe this was more serious than she thought. "I don't know what was in that bag, sir."

Cates sighed. "Been there, heard that, Monica."

"That man looked so miserable lying there in all that filth," she recounted. "I just thought I'd tidy up a bit before I went on to Illinois. Cheer him up. Help him make a new start." She felt herself becoming suddenly agitated. "You know, I really have to be somewhere. Is this going to take much longer?" The woman in Illinois was a kindergarten teacher. No telling how many lives would be affected if Monica were late for her assignment. Maybe Tess had gone on ahead. She hoped so.

Cates leaned toward her. "Do you understand that you have been arrested on the charge of drug trafficking?"

Monica nodded. "I do now. Thank goodness we've got it all straightened out."

"We don't have anything straightened out, lady." Cates seemed to be growing impatient. "Now forget this fairy tale about Illinois and the wrong house and Tess the mystery chick. You were caught with two kilos of cocaine at 3:00 A.M. this morning. What's that all about? Are you a dealer or a buyer?"

Monica shook her head. She had to admit, it looked bad. How could she ever convince him of the truth? "You don't understand," she began. "I was only there because . . ." She hesitated.

"Yeah?" Cates stood up. He paced slowly around the table, stopping just behind her chair where he stood over his alleged drug runner in a threatening stance. "Go on," he said.

And the truth shall set you free. She heard the words over and over in her head. She had said them countless times to help others who were caught in the fallout of lies and deception. Now she needed God's words herself. Still, she had nothing to offer the detective, but the truth.

"Because . . . well, you see, I'm . . . an angel."

The next morning Monica sat at yet another table across from yet another stranger, the police department's chief consulting psychiatrist, Dr. Ray Arnovitz. The bespectacled young man was studying a piece of paper in front of him with scribbling all over it. She could read the bold print upside down: Psychiatric Evaluation Form. Underneath that were the words: Name: "Doe, Monica. Address: unknown. Age: unknown." The charges pending against her were clear: possession of narcotics for sales/cocaine. Dr. Arnovitz was the psychiatrist assigned to evaluate her mental condition.

"Does being an angel distress you?" he asked, waving a fly away from the evaluation form.

Monica still couldn't believe this was happening, that it had gone this far. But again, she could only be honest with those who seemed so desperate for answers. They were only doing their jobs, she guessed, just as she was last night when it had all started.

"Well, taking human form can throw you sometimes, but all in all, it's marvelous." She hoped that would satisfy him.

"And how long have you been an angel?" he asked.

"All my life."

The doctor's pencil was poised over the blank under *Age*. "And how long is that?"

"Forever." Monica smiled at the doctor.

The doctor gave her a kind of crooked smile back. "Have you sold drugs 'forever'?"

"No!" She couldn't believe he would suggest such a thing. "Angels would never, ever do that!"

"Ah, so you're not an angel when you're selling drugs?" The doctor seemed to think he was onto something.

"Yes! No!" Was he purposely trying to confuse her?

—A DESPONDENT MONICA FINDS HERSELF IN THE COUNTY JAIL

Dr. Arnovitz removed his glasses and studied her for a moment. "Do you understand why you're here today?" he asked.

"Yes." At least she knew the answer to this one. "Because I didn't leave when Tess told me to."

"And who is Tess?"

"She's an angel, too."

"Like you?"

"No, she's taller."

The doctor sat back in his chair. Then he leaned over the evaluation form and began writing furiously. Somehow Monica knew she hadn't convinced the doctor of her sanity and this wasn't over yet. She sighed and wondered where Tess was at this moment. Why had no one arrived to help her?

A guard led Monica to a communal cell full of boisterous, complaining, and crying women. She found a corner where she curled up on the floor, and keeping one eye open for any sign of Tess, she tried to rest.

The next morning she was re-cuffed and transported along with several of her fellow inmates to the criminal courts building to wait in line for her turn at justice. Each of the prisoners wore a neon orange jumpsuit with the word "County" across the shoulders. This was too humiliating for words.

Judge Stanley Webster's court bustled with activity. Monica watched the lawyers in their dark suits as they hurried back and forth taking care of last-minute business. A uniformed bailiff stood talking to a court reporter, while a myriad of troubled family members waited impatiently for the release of their loved ones. The lack of a friendly face made Monica increasingly uneasy. She knew God was with her, but she wanted to see Tess walk in the door. Monica was afraid that her absence could only mean trouble ahead.

"All rise," the bailiff said in a lifeless voice. He'd obviously been doing this a while. "Case number C94 dash 20675, People versus Melinda Caron. Prostitution, possession of a controlled substance, resisting arrest."

While Melinda's defender and an assistant DA discussed the terms of her plea with Judge Webster, Monica's eyes circled the courtroom again for Tess. In the row directly behind her, she could hear two attorneys arguing in low tones.

"I don't care what you've got on him," the African-American attorney said to the female attorney sitting beside him. "I've got a warrant with the wrong day, the wrong middle name, and a client with a broken arm who says he had two good ones when he walked into interrogation."

Monica gasped. That was terrible.

"And I've got a twenty-year-old girl at St. Mark's who'd swear she used to have a complete skull before Diaz dragged her into a parking lot. That is, she'd swear it if she could speak."

Monica could hardly control herself. Humans could be so . . . so violent to one another.

"I'll make you a deal. I've got a 'three strikes' coming up. Two prior assaults. Third strike was breaking into a candy machine. Can't send my guy away for that. Drop the charges, I'll give you the warrant, and Diaz pleads battery on the St. Mark's girl."

Monica tensed.

"Case dismissed," Webster announced. "Next case. Let's keep things moving." He motioned to the bailiff to hurry it up.

"Case number 20699," clipped the bailiff. "People versus Monica Doe. Charged with possession of cocaine for sale with intent to distribute."

The words sent a chill down Monica's neck. As an angel, she was a force for good. It was preposterous to think that an angel could have any involvement with something as poisonous as cocaine.

At the bailiff's instruction, Monica stood and approached the bench. The middle-aged judge reviewed the paperwork in a manila file folder, then studied her a moment before speaking.

"Ms. Monica . . . Doe?" the judge said. "You have no last name?"

"No, Your Honor. Not officially."

"Do you have legal representation?"

"Uh, no, I . . ." She hesitated and looked around the courtroom once again just to be sure. It seemed only reasonable that Tess would either show up herself or send someone to untangle this legal mess. How could an angel in prison be any good to anyone?

Then the double doors opened and in walked Sam. He wore a well-cut suit, conservative tie, and carried a designer attaché case embossed with the letters "AITOGT." He was an imposing individual, this Sam, the "Angel in Times of Great Trouble." Monica could have cried out with delight. He was just the angel she needed right then. She knew she could depend on Tess.

"Yes, Your Honor." Monica clasped her hands and smiled up at the judge. "Here's my attorney now."

"Where?" the judge asked.

Sam walked up to stand beside her. She put her arm through his. "Right here," she said proudly, then turned to Sam. "I knew they'd send somebody. I'm *so* glad it's you."

Monica looked happily up at the judge only to see him frowning.

SAM (PAUL WINFIELD) ARRIVES IN THE COURTROOM

"Monica, I'm not here to represent you," Sam said. "You went to the wrong address, and now you've set a serious chain of events into motion. We have to let them play out."

"But, Sam, something's wrong. I can't seem to do anything except *be* here. All my gifts are gone. You're the first contact I've had with anyone in the realm."

"And the last for a while, I'm afraid," Sam said softly.

"Ms. Doe, I'll ask again." Monica became dimly aware of the judge's voice. "Do you have any representation?"

She was suddenly aware that everyone in the courtroom was staring at her with mixed looks of amusement and pity. She realized then that Sam was invisible to everyone but her.

Sam shook his head.

"I . . . I guess not," she said slowly, feeling very alone all of a sudden.

As Sam walked back up the aisle, he stopped and turned back around. "God turns everything around all the time, so something good's got to come of this. I just can't tell you when, that's all. And remember, He'll never leave or forsake you. Even just because you're stuck in human form, that doesn't mean you're not an angel."

"Well, of course I'm an angel!" Monica announced confidently. No matter what would befall her in this snafu about drugs and dealing, Monica would never doubt that she was an angel.

"Ms. Doe?"

The judge had her full attention. "Yes, Your Honor?"

"As your file indicates no visible means of support, and you have no visible counsel present, the court will therefore appoint a public defender to represent you."

"Thank you very much, Your Honor."

"No matter what happens, never forget who you are. Never." And with that, Sam disappeared.

"Is there a public defender or someone from legal aid present in the courtroom?" the judge asked.

A hand in the back of the room waved wildly in the air. It was the woman attorney Monica had heard arguing earlier with the male attorney. "Yes, Your Honor. Jake Stone is here and available."

Jake hurried up to the bench. "I'm not here really, Judge," he said smoothly. "Not in a formal capacity anyway. I just dropped by to confer briefly with Assistant District Attorney Sue Cheney and, actually, that can wait, so . . ." He clutched his paperwork close to his side and turned to leave.

"Stone, you're on this case," Judge Webster said firmly.

"Your Honor, if I may—"

"Order!" Webster commanded. "Miss Cheney?"

"This is pretty cut-and-dried," Sue Cheney told the judge and an obviously miffed Jake Stone. "The defendant was arrested last night during a SWAT operation. She was carrying two kilos, denies any connection, and get this, insists she's an angel. Two psychiatric evaluations, and both concur. The county will recommend release to State Mental on a five to fifteen with a guilty but mentally ill."

Jake grabbed the file from the prosecutor for a quick once-over. "She's that nutty?" he said.

"As my mother-in-law's fruitcake," she responded dryly. "Just make your motion and let's get outta here."

Jake gave Ms. Cheney a wry smile. "It's a funny habit of mine. I like to actually meet the people I help commit to a mental institution."

The prosecutor raised her eyebrows. "Careful, you'll start taking home rapists and lost puppies pretty soon."

"You've got two minutes," the judge told Jake Stone.

Jake walked toward Monica, who had been following all of this intently. "Ms. Doe?" he said.

"It's awfully nice of you to jump into the fray like this." She smiled and extended her hand.

"Yes, well it's gonna be a short fray. Look, they've got you cold here. If you plead innocent you go to trial and the jury's going to send you up for fifteen years to life."

"Life?" Monica pondered that for a moment. "That could be awfully long in my case."

Jake gave her a sidewise glance. "Right. Now, if you plead 'guilty but mentally ill,' the nice judge over there will let you go to the state mental hospital where you'll maybe only spend five years, fifteen tops. And you can get all better at the same time."

She stared at him. "Better?"

"They can help you handle your problem."

For some reason Monica felt two feet high. "My only problem is that nobody believes me," she said indignantly. "Of course, you believe me, don't you? You're my lawyer."

"Being your lawyer doesn't mean I believe you, Ms. Doe," Jake said. "As a matter of fact, I hardly believe any of my clients, or anybody else for that matter."

Monica suddenly felt very sorry for this poor human. "You must be a very unhappy man," she said.

Jake seemed surprised by her comment. She turned to the judge. "Your Honor, sir? Mr. Judge?"

"Ms. Doe—" Jake tried to stop her.

"I'm not crazy, Judge, really, I'm not," she said. "And I don't want to be put away. I want a fair chance to have a trial and tell my side of things. I know who and what I am!"

"You have the right to a competency hearing if you wish, Ms. Doe," the judge said kindly.

"No," Jake said. "That's not a good idea at all."

The judge ignored him. "Now, if you are found competent, you must then stand trial, and frankly, young lady, the evidence against you is heavy."

Monica nodded. "I understand. But I'm not crazy."

"How do you want to handle this, Stone?" Judge Webster asked the public defender.

Jake studied Monica for a moment.

"Believe somebody," she pleaded. "Just this once?"

"You don't have a real trial to prepare for right now anyway, Jake," Sue interjected with a smirk. "Except maybe that deposition with Dr. Seagram."

Jake rubbed his eyes, closed Monica's file, and took a long, deep breath. The kind of breath one took before diving off a springboard for the first time. The kind of breath that said "This will feel great when it's over."

"Your Honor, my client and I move to controvert the findings of the state," he said.

Sue shook her head in disbelief.

"Okay, then, a hearing to establish competence will be held, let's see, Thursday in this court at 1:00 P.M.," Judge Webster pronounced. "The prisoner is temporarily remanded to the custody of the state mental hospital until that time. Next case."

Monica beamed and turned to Jake. "God bless you, Jacob Stone."

The lawyer pointed his finger at her. "Don't even start with me about God," he shot back. "I do not for one minute believe you are an angel."

Monica shrugged as a police officer led her out of the courtroom.

Monica's wrists were red and sore from the tightly cinched handcuffs she'd worn for at least five hours now. The best part of arriving at the state's mental facility was when Pete, the tall, heavyset orderly, met her at the door and freed her hands.

She peered into a nearby room and saw a number of blue-robed patients wandering aimlessly around. One seemed to be chasing something, while another huddled in a corner, moaning. Monica jumped back as a tall woman looked out at her and hissed.

"Don't worry," Pete said kindly. "You'll get used to it." He turned to a woman who was kneeling in front of a fire extinguisher, her hands folded in prayer. "Hey Rosie, I've got an angel for you!"

"And He shall give His angels charge over thee!" Rosie spoke directly at the fire extinguisher as if reciting a sacred canon. She rose to her feet, put an index finger to her lips, and touched places on the wall around the extinguisher in a well-practiced ritual.

"We've got all types," Pete told her as he led her down the hall. "Religious nuts, schizos, delusionals."

Monica winced. How had he labeled her? "I guess that's what everyone thinks I am," she said.

"Yeah, well, angels are a dime a dozen around here."

They stopped at Room 23 and Pete knocked quietly. "Claire," he said. "I've got a roommate for you." He turned to

Monica. "I thought you'd want to bunk with a coworker." He winked at her and opened the door. Inside, a frightened woman sat in the corner of a twin bed next to a padlocked window. Her knees were drawn up to her chin. The other bed was vacant and neatly made up with white sheets and a dark gray thermal blanket. Pete took Monica's arm and led her into the room.

"Mayday, Mayday," the woman screamed, cowering further back into the corner.

"Nothin' personal." Pete cocked his head toward Monica. "She says that all the time." He turned back to Claire. "Claire, calm down! This is Monica. She's going to sleep right here in this bunk. There's nothing to be afraid of. She's an angel, too." He chuckled. "Just like you."

Monica looked at Pete in surprise. "Claire . . . is an angel?"

"Mayday, Mayday, Mayday," Claire continued, louder and faster.

Pete rolled his eyes. "That's what she says." He shrugged. "She thinks she's an angel. You think you're an angel, so you've already got a lot in common." Pete patted Monica on the shoulder and closed the door behind him.

"Mayday! Mayday! Mayday!" Claire said over and over.

Monica looked around the miserable room with its fingerprinted windows, grimy floor, and terrified occupant. So this was what crazy looked like. How could they have ever used that word to describe her?

Jake Stone returned from the men's room at The Sidebar to see Sue Cheney and another woman taking a seat at the crowded bar. This downtown restaurant was popular with lawyers who worked in the county courthouse or practiced in a nearby office building. Tonight it seemed unusually packed, smoke-filled, and loud.

Jake came up behind Sue. "You're sitting on my jacket," he said.

She turned to smile coyly at him. "I would have guessed that your stool was marked with a plaque or something."

Okay, so Jake drank a little, it was common knowledge. Needling him about it was just part of their routine.

"Only three days until Monica Doe's hearing and we don't have the discovery from your office." Jake knew the best way to get around Sue was to cut to the chase.

"Oh, Monica the angel?" she jeered.

Jake gave her a menacing look as he swept up his coat from the back of her chair. "I want that discovery in the morning," he said firmly.

In legal circles, Jake was viewed as heartless and distant, even with clients. He had once thrived on getting his street scum clients a suspended sentence and then moving them back into society for another chance. Now he cut his deals quickly and was off to a gin and tonic before 4:30. Jake didn't consider himself an alcoholic. He simply relied on a few drinks to wear off the edges of a day in court. Sure, some personal losses had affected his life, but he was never one for self-reflection.

Sue would take what Jake dished out and then serve it right back. She was a solid strategist, but preferred duking it out in front of a jury rather than slogging through the preliminary negotiations, compromises, and favors many criminal cases required.

"Done," she said. "You'll want to listen carefully to the arrest tapes. They're quite entertaining."

Just then, a woman came up alongside Jake and grabbed his elbow. "Sorry I'm late," she said, and greeted everyone by name.

"Thanks for coming." Jake motioned to a nearby table. "Let's sit over there."

"I didn't know shrinks made house calls," Sue said.

Jake ignored her, picked up his drink, and followed Ellen Shrader toward the booth. He tried to put Sue's reference to his drinking out of his mind. Also, he didn't appreciate that she had now seen him with Dr. Shrader. Sue would put two and two together and know that they were meeting to discuss Monica Doe.

"Why the rush to talk tonight?" Ellen slid into one side of the booth. The Sidebar had just completed a major renovation and the traditional dark interior had given way to soft hues of umber and celadon. Between running into Sue Cheney and the chic ambiance, Jake wasn't sure he'd made such a good choice in restaurants tonight.

"I've got a competency hearing on Thursday," Jake told Ellen. "I really need you to evaluate Monica Doe and testify."

"Thursday? And you're calling me now?"

"It happened fast. The woman was arrested in a dealer's house holding two kilos. Says she was at the right address, wrong state."

"Wrong state?" Ellen shook her head. "You can't commit somebody for bad grades in geography."

"She says she's an angel," Jake added, as if that fact would somehow clear Ellen's appointment book.

"And you're going to defend that?" Ellen looked at him as if he were the one needing an evaluation.

"I only have to prove she's competent to stand trial," he said, staring down into his drink. Sometimes he wished he were a janitor. It would be so much easier dealing with brooms than with people.

Monica paced back and forth across the eight-by-nine-foot room she shared with her lunatic roommate.

"The funny thing is," she said, "I'm sure I heard Jacksonville, Florida. It's so disturbing because I've never made a mistake like that before. Oh, I've made mistakes. Angels, real angels, aren't perfect." She looked over at Claire still huddled on her bed. "You know, Claire, it's okay to admit you're not a real angel. God loves you just the way you are." Monica approached the other woman and gently placed her hand over Claire's clenched fingers.

"Mayday!" Claire cried, jerking her hand away.

The door flew open and Pete entered the room followed by a nurse in a stiff white uniform. She carried a small tray which held a hypodermic needle.

Claire shook her head with recognition and acceptance. "Bye-bye, angel," Claire said sweetly to Monica. "Bye-bye."

Monica turned her head. She couldn't look.

Jake and Ellen passed a woman genuflecting before a fire extinguisher, as they followed Pete down the hall the following morning. They entered the dayroom where most of the patients watched an *Andy of Mayberry* rerun on TV or stared blankly out the window.

"She's over there." Pete pointed to a far corner of the room.

Monica stood by the window, a frenzied look in her eyes. Jake glanced nervously at Ellen as they approached the young

THE MEDICATION WHICH CALMS HUMANS ONLY
SPINS MONICA OUT OF CONTROL

woman. He was relieved to be in the company of a trained professional.

"What do you want?" she spat at them. "Who are you? Leave me alone! Go away!"

"She wasn't like this yesterday," Jake said, puzzled at his client's strange behavior. The charming Irish lilt was gone, and her voice was now distinctly American.

"Maybe she was playing nice yesterday," Ellen suggested. "One day she's an angel, and the next day she's . . ."

"Never forget who you are!" Monica spoke now in the voice of an upperclass Englishwoman. "Just because you're stuck in human form doesn't mean you're not an angel."

Jake shrugged at Dr. Shrader, feeling like he should apologize for what he had asked her to do for his client.

Monica tossed her head back to look out the window again, then turned toward them once more. She pointed her right index finger and spoke as if delivering a curse. "You don't know who you're dealing with here. I could break you like that!" She snapped her fingers.

"Monica, have you been given any medication?" Dr. Shrader asked.

Tears suddenly puddled in Monica's eyes, and she almost looked like the woman Jake had seen in the courtroom the day before. "Yes, help me," she pleaded.

"They can't do that," Jake blurted.

"I'm afraid they can," Ellen said. "If she's drugged, no comprehensive evaluation is possible."

"Okay, look, if I can get a court order to stop the medication, how soon can you talk to her?" Jake just wanted the bizarre case against Monica Doe behind him.

"That depends on what kind of drug it is and when they administered it," Ellen told him. "Maybe twenty-four hours."

"Ha!" Monica laughed wickedly, twisting her long auburn hair around her finger. "Twenty-four hours? Too late! I'll be long gone by then!"

The Sidebar may have updated its decor, but it still felt like home to Jake. The strange episode at the hospital with Monica was behind him, and he had acquired the court order late that afternoon. Now he needed a drink. The bartenders at The Sidebar knew him by name, and he appreciated that his "usual" was always poured and stirred between when he walked through the door and when he found a stool.

He sat down and immediately spread out the discovery papers, psychiatric reports, a cassette tape, and a blurry photo of Monica's palm. He couldn't quite make out the words written on her hand and decided to ask the white-suited stranger

————— SAM OFFERS ADVICE TO MONICA'S LAWYER, JAKE STONE (JOE MORTON)

sitting next to him for a candid opinion. Little did Jake realize that this stranger was Sam, the Special Agent Angel.

"Excuse me, sir, sorry to bother you." Jake held the
photo out in front of him. "Can you read what's written on
this hand here?"

The man brought Jake's hand closer to his face and studied Monica's open palm in the photo. "801 Cedar. Jacksonville. Tough neighborhood. Evidence, is it?" he asked.

This guy must come into The Sidebar often enough to
understand the profile of its clientele.

Jake nodded. "A client of mine. Claims she's an angel."

"An angel? Imagine that."

A bartender set a mug of steaming coffee in front of the
man. "Thanks," he said. "Nothing like a good cup of Joe."

"I haven't heard that since the Army," Jake said.

"Korea?"

"'Nam. Saigon actually. Near the end."

The man nodded. "Hard thing to carry around with you," he said.

Jake frowned slightly. "Harder to let go of," he said.

"Maybe that angel of yours could help," the stranger suggested.

"Nah. She's nuts."

"Then why are you defending her?" the man asked.

Good question. "I'm always drawn to the impossible," Jake said with a smile.

"With God, all things are possible," the man said softly. "You know, I've met a lot of men who don't believe in angels, but I never met a man who didn't want to." The stranger took a sip of his coffee.

Jake studied him for a moment. The man was an older, wiser warrior. Jake liked him. But the moment was over when Ellen suddenly appeared at his side.

"I thought I might find you here," she said, pulling out the stool beside him.

Jake smiled a greeting. "Ellen, sit down. This is—" He turned back to his new acquaintance so he could introduce him to Ellen, but the man's stool was empty. That fast. Jake looked around, but he was nowhere in sight. He shook his head. "Never mind."

Ellen picked up the photo of Monica's hand while Jake motioned to the waiter to bring them two glasses of wine.

"She told me about this," Ellen said.

Jake was pleasantly surprised. "You talked to her already?"

Ellen shrugged. "I stopped at the hospital after work, just to see if the meds had worn off."

Jake leaned toward her. "So, what do you think?"

"Jake, I'll give you my honest opinion," she hesitated, "but I'm telling you up front, I don't want to testify for her."

Joe frowned. "Well, why? What happened?"

"Nothing. Once she was off the psychotropics, she was fine. And I mean, fine." Ellen's face grew more serious. "She's the most sane person I've ever met."

"Except for one minor matter. She thinks she's an angel."

"Yes. She's either the craziest woman in the world, or she's who she says she is."

Jake was caught off guard. He would never have expected this from a medical professional like Dr. Shrader. "You're honestly telling me you believe she's an angel?" he asked a little too loudly. The waiter looked at them wide-eyed as he set the two glasses in front of them.

Ellen took a sip of wine. "I'm saying that nothing makes her delusional, except that she thinks she's an angel. She makes more sense than my dentist, and he's convinced he'll win the lottery on April Fool's Day in 1998. My neighbor dresses up like Madonna and pretends her hairbrush is a microphone. Who's delusional?"

Delusional was one thing, but competent to stand trial was another. What was Ellen saying?

"So, is she competent or not?"

Ellen sighed. "Take away the angel factor, yes. But I'm not going to get up in court and say that. I'd be laughed out of the business."

"All you've got to say," Jake argued, "is that she understands the charges and can assist in her defense."

"Her defense is being an angel. But you try to prove that, and you'll be out of a job, too." Ellen finished her drink and stood up to leave. "I'm afraid you're going to lose this one, Jake."

Jake took her words as a personal challenge. "And what exactly do you mean by that?"

"Nobody wants this to go to trial," Ellen said plainly. "Nobody wants those kinds of headlines. 'Webster Declares Heavenly Visitor Is Competent.' 'Will DA Prosecute or Persecute Lost Angel?' Look, I've got to run. I'm sorry."

"Nobody wants this to go to trial," Jake repeated thoughtfully. He gave Ellen's hand a lame squeeze and turned back to his drink. Then he dropped the tape into the tape recorder, punched the play button, and listened once again to Monica's account of what happened on Cedar Street.

"My hearing is tomorrow, Claire." Monica stared out the window into the black night.

"Mayday."

"If I win, I won't be coming back here. So I want you to know that I'm glad I met you and . . ."

Claire stared straight ahead. "Bye-bye, angel. Bye-bye. Bye-bye."

A white dove landed on the windowsill outside of Judge Webster's courtroom. Monica was grateful for the graceful creature's presence, a symbol that God was watching over her.

"As we entered the apartment, I saw a Caucasian female holding Exhibit A."

Monica directed her attention back to Detective Cates who was testifying in the hearing today to determine her competency to stand trial. Except for the judge, counsel, defendant, and witnesses, the courtroom was empty.

"Can you identify that female?" Sue Cheney's list of questions was extensive and her witnesses rehearsed.

"Yes, absolutely." Detective Cates pointed boldly at the accused. "There she is."

"Your Honor, please let the record show that Detective Cates has identified the defendant, Monica Doe." She stepped back and then forward, looking as if she were a ballet dancer about to do a pirouette. "And did you then interrogate this suspect?"

"Yes." The detective nodded vehemently. "She admitted to having the cocaine in her possession at the time of her arrest. She refused to give her full name and she had no identification." He cleared his throat. "She kept saying she was an angel."

"Thank you, Detective Cates." She turned to Jake Stone. "Your witness."

Jake approached the witness stand. "Detective Cates, was Monica Doe's name on your warrant?"

"No, sir."

"Were you surprised to find her there?"

"Well, yes."

"Did she offer any explanation?"

"She said she was at the wrong address." Detective Cates rolled his eyes. "She said that she and someone named Tess were supposed to help a kindergarten teacher who was going to leave her husband."

"Uh-huh. And did you check into her alibi?"

"That she's an angel? Are you kidding? I had her," the detective boasted. "I had the cocaine. I'm not interested in Illinois. I'm interested in the state of Florida."

"And I'm interested in justice," Jake came back with fire in his eyes. "Thank you very much."

"Ms. Cheney, call your next witness," the judge ordered.

"Dr. Ray Arnovitz."

Monica smiled as the doctor took the stand. He was the one person so far that she thought might believe her story, even a little. "He was very nice," she said to Jake. "I enjoyed our little chats."

Arnovitz stated his name and professional qualifications for the court.

"Dr. Arnovitz, have you examined Monica Doe?" Sue Cheney asked.

"Yes, I have."

"And in your expert opinion, is she competent to understand the charges against her?"

"Monica Doe suffers from delusions and hallucinations, as well as an altered sense of self," he began. "In her delusional state, believing that she is an angel, it is my opinion that she might very well consider herself above the law."

Monica jumped to her feet. "No! We always honor the law! Always!" So much for thinking Dr. Arnovitz understood or believed in her.

"Counsel—restrain your client!" Judge Webster ordered.

Jake pulled Monica back into her chair. "You're not helping," he whispered fiercely.

"What treatment would you recommend for someone diagnosed as delusional, Doctor?" Cheney asked her witness.

"A stringent pattern of psychotropic drugs in a psychiatric hospital."

Monica gasped and opened her mouth, but Jake gripped her arm.

"In her naive state," the doctor went on, "incarceration could put her life in jeopardy."

Cheney thanked Dr. Arnovitz, and he was about to leave the stand when Jake stopped him. "Excuse me, Doctor, I have a few questions," he said. "Now, it's your opinion that incarcerating Monica Doe would put her life in jeopardy?"

"Yes."

"But a stringent pattern of psychotropic drugs in a mental institution would not?"

"Of course not," he stated, seeming offended that Jake would question his judgment.

"What happens to a schizophrenic patient who takes psychotropic drugs?" Jake pressed.

"Many become more balanced and able to connect in a healthy manner with reality," Dr. Arnovitz replied.

"What happens when a person who is not psychotic takes them?"

Where was Jake Stone going with this? Monica wondered. She really needed him to hurry things along so she could get to Illinois.

"A mentally stable person might become slightly depressed," the doctor answered with a touch of impatience. "Otherwise, nothing."

"Nothing?" Jake feigned surprise. "When Monica Doe was given this medication, what was her reaction?"

Arnovitz shifted on the stand.

"Feel free to consult your notes," Jake said.

Dr. Arnovitz put on a pair of reading glasses, opened an accordion file, removed a report, and scanned through some papers. "Well . . . I didn't personally examine Monica Doe after administering."

"So, Doctor, you don't know whether Monica's reaction to psychotropic drugs is that of a normal human being or not."

Dr. Arnovitz frowned slightly. "No."

Jake nodded to Dr. Arnovitz. "Thank you, Doctor. That was very helpful."

Monica didn't think Dr. Arnovitz cared about helping Jake. She didn't know much about legal trials and such, but she could tell that much.

Judge Webster turned to Sue Cheney.

"The prosecution rests, Your Honor," she said.

Monica thought the attorney looked a little pale. Maybe she wasn't feeling well.

Jake rose to his feet then and called Dr. Ellen Shrader as his first witness. "She was subpoenaed this morning, and I ask the court to declare her a hostile witness."

Monica gave Ellen a warm smile, but Ellen didn't see her. She was too busy glaring at Jake as she took the witness stand.

"Dr. Shrader," Jake began, "after examining Monica Doe, what is your expert opinion of her mental state?"

"I found her to be responsive, lucid, and alert," she said in a clipped tone.

"Doctor, let me give you a hypothetical situation." Jake looked thoughtful for a moment. "If Monica had told you she was a . . . well, maybe a plumber, is there anything about her behavior that would lead you to believe she was insane?"

Ellen smiled. "No."

"So, if we substituted the word *plumber* for *angel* and if she said she'd gone to the wrong address to fix a toilet instead of a soul—would you consider her delusional or just directionally impaired?"

"I would not consider her delusional," the psychiatrist answered.

"Just one more question," Jake said. "Do you believe in angels yourself?"

"No, I do not," she answered.

"Can you prove, however, that they do not exist?"

"The witness is not an expert in angelology, Your Honor," Sue Cheney interrupted Jake's questioning.

"Who is?" he fired back. "No further questions."

"No questions," Cheney added.

"The defense calls Theresa Hayman," he announced.

Dr. Shrader stepped down from the witness stand and smiled at Monica as she headed toward the back of the room.

"I call Theresa Marie Hayman," Jake said.

"Who?" Monica couldn't hide her surprise. She watched as a woman, dressed in the kind of knit outfit that packs well and is perfect for travel, entered from the back of the courtroom. She'd never seen this woman before. Why hadn't Jake told her about her, whoever she was? She eyed her suspiciously as the bailiff swore her in and she took the stand.

"State your full name and address, please," Jake said.

"Theresa Marie Hayman. 801 Cedar Street, Jacksonville, Illinois."

Monica beamed. Jake had found the kindergarten teacher. Did that mean that her attorney now believed her story?

"Ms. Hayman, can you please tell us what happened to you on the evening of March the second?"

Terry Hayman smoothed down her skirt and sat up a little straighter. "I was planning to leave my husband . . . for someone else. I packed and called a cab. The driver was a woman named Tess."

Monica liked this lady.

"When I got in the cab, she was holding something, a drawing my four-year-old had made of our family. I couldn't imagine how she got it. Then there was this incredible light. I don't know where it came from, but it was beautiful and it filled the entire cab. It was all around me."

Everyone in the courtroom was listening intently as Terry spoke. Jake looked especially pleased.

"Then Tess told me some things about myself, things I knew but had forgotten—that my husband and children loved me and needed me—that God loved me. I started crying, then turned around and walked back into my home . . ."

"Did this Tess have any explanation for all this?" Jake asked.

"Yes . . . I know this sounds crazy, but . . . she told me she was an angel. She said she was sorry she wasn't there sooner, but she was filling in for another angel who'd been . . . how did she put it? Detained."

"And did she identify that angel by name?" Jake prodded.

"Tess called her Monica."

"Thank heavens Tess made it!" Monica blurted.

"No further questions," Jake said.

Sue Cheney stepped up to the witness then. "Ms. Hayman, have you ever met Monica Doe?" she asked, gesturing to Monica.

"No, I haven't," Terry answered, and seemed to shrink back from the aggressive attorney.

"Do you know if she's an angel?"

"An angel? No . . . no, I don't."

"Then you really don't know anything about her, do you?"

"No."

"Your Honor, may we approach?"

The judge nodded, and the three of them huddled together for a sidebar. Monica listened closely.

"Your Honor, I move to have this witness's testimony stricken from the record. It's completely immaterial to the competency of Monica Doe."

"That's not true at all," Monica said aloud. "It's entirely relevant."

They ignored her.

"Your Honor, it's completely relevant to establishing my client's credibility," Jake insisted.

Go, Jake! Monica cheered to herself.

"As an angel?" Judge Webster gave Jake a stern look. "Jake, you are not going to retry *Miracle on 34th Street* in my courtroom."

"This is not about Santa Claus, Your Honor. This is about a young woman's life. If you will allow me to put her on the stand, I will prove that she fulfills all the competency requirements. She understands the charges . . ."

"I do!" Monica said loudly so that they couldn't ignore her this time. "Possession with intent to distribute. Mandatory fifteen to twenty-five in the pen!"

Jake waved a hand at her furiously, then turned back to the judge. "She is able to assist in her defense."

The judge was looking a little upset. "Are you telling me if she goes to trial, you will put angels on trial as well?"

Jake cocked his head and stared at the judge. "Are you saying you don't want this to go to trial because . . . what? You don't believe in angels? 'In God We Trust,' but angels we're not so sure about? It's gonna be some trial."

DO YOU SWEAR TO TELL THE TRUTH,
THE WHOLE TRUTH, SO HELP YOU GOD?

"I need to think about this," the judge said, shaking his head. "Step back. I will examine the defendant myself." He downed a glass of water the observant bailiff held out to him, reviewed the files quietly, then assumed a somber gaze as he turned to Monica. "Ms. Doe?"

Monica rose, stepped up to the bailiff, and placed one hand on the Bible. He swore her in and she proudly took her place on the witness stand. It was about time.

"Ms. Doe, a moment ago, you repeated the formal charges against you. Now, I would like you to tell me what they mean."

This would be easier than she thought. "Well, Detective Cates and his fellows dropped in on the man in the bed and arrested him and me, too, because I was holding the bag that they say had some drugs in it. They thought I was going to sell them to the man in the bed, if you can believe it. An angel dealing drugs." She giggled.

The judge wasn't laughing. "Were you?" he asked.

"No, of course not! That would be crazy, which is kinda funny, 'cause that's what the doctors think I am, but of course I'm not."

"But you think you're an angel," the judge affirmed.

"Well, I am. So if I didn't think I was, then I would be crazy. Why is it," she asked, "when you talk to God, you're praying, but when God talks to you, you're nuts?"

Out of the corner of her eye, she saw Jake smile.

But the judge sighed. "Court is adjourned for one hour," he announced, striking his gavel. He then turned and disappeared into his chambers.

After conferring with Sue Cheney for a moment, Jake returned to his client. "Webster will be back in an hour and entertain a motion to dismiss, just watch," Jake said confidently. "He'd rather drop the charges than put an angel on trial in front of the whole world. We're going to win and you're going to walk out of here, Ms. Doe."

Monica was ecstatic. Could this mess really be about over? "Do they have coffee somewhere?" she asked.

"I didn't know angels drank coffee," Jake said, smiling.

"How would you know?" Monica returned his smile. "You don't even believe in angels."

He nodded. "That's right, I don't."

Monica suddenly felt let down. Sure, she would be thrilled if the judge dismissed the case and she could be free once again, but then . . . what was the purpose? What had it all meant? "It means a lot, you getting me out of all this trouble," she said slowly. "But it would mean a lot more if you did it because you believed I am who I say I am. In a strange way, I feel I've failed."

Jake looked at her, really looked at her for the first time. It was almost as if he were trying to see right into her soul. She'd gotten his attention. For now, that had to be enough.

Jake went to get them some coffee, while everyone else filed out of the courtroom. In a moment Jake returned, two steaming cups of coffee in his hands. He held one out to her, then sat down beside her.

"You know, I used to pray for an angel when I was in 'Nam," he said slowly. "We all did. I would hear guys screaming for them, children begging for them. But they never came. There were no angels in Saigon."

"How do you know that for sure?" Monica asked.

"No angel could see what I saw and not put a stop to it," Jake said bitterly. "Even God abandoned us."

Monica decided to grab what she could. "So, you do believe in God?"

"Just enough to really hate the guy."

"You blame God for the evil that others create?"

"I blame Him for not stopping it," Jake said.

Monica remembered what Sam had told her. "Sometimes things get set in motion that must be played out. I'm learning that myself. God's timing is not our timing."

But Jake just shook his head and waved her off. "Save your breath. If I needed a lesson in angels, I'd go to Sunday school." He looked at her closely now. "You want to know what real angels look like? They look like Claire."

"Claire?" Did he mean—what was he saying?

"She was this nurse I knew in Saigon. I never knew where she came from, but she always showed up just when we needed her. So, it's the fall of Saigon, the very last day. We're all on a roof, scrambling to get into the last helicopter out before the Cong came in. It was everything you've ever imagined hell to be. Screaming, terrified people climbing over each other to get into the chopper. I was the last on the rope ladder, carrying a little girl, daughter of a Vietnamese lieutenant. He was my friend . . ." Jake rubbed his eyes. "Before he died, he made me promise to take May Ling to America." He smiled, remembering. "We called her Mayday 'cause she was always getting into some kind of trouble."

Monica stared at him, stunned. "Mayday?" she repeated.

"I had a good grip on that kid," he went on. "But the crowds . . . somebody actually tried to pull her back down. The chopper's taking off, they're pulling up the ladder, and she falls. Back into the crowd. Into Claire's arms. I couldn't believe it. I wanted to jump off, but we were too high, and they weren't going back. Claire held Mayday in her arms and waved, smiling. And I knew Claire had chosen to stay. To help. Even though . . ." He stopped, unable to go on. Monica put a hand on his arm. "Even though," he finally choked out, "she knew she would die. That, Monica, is a real angel."

"I know," she said thoughtfully. "Now I know."

Jake and Monica sat without speaking for several moments until finally, one by one, the others trickled back into the courtroom. Jake mopped his forehead with a handkerchief as Sue Cheney returned to her table, and the bailiff announced Judge Webster. But Monica found it difficult to keep her mind on what was going on here. She couldn't stop thinking about Jake and Claire and—

"Look at his face." Jake brought Monica back to reality. "He wants the charges dropped. I can tell. I'm good at this."

Monica frowned. Something bigger was going on. She knew that now.

"The court has considered Ms. Doe's rather interesting explanation for her presence during a police action," the judge began. "However, the court also acknowledges the state's inability to disprove her explanation."

"This is great," Jake whispered.

"As the court cannot disprove the existence of angels," Judge Webster continued, "it therefore cannot use 'angelhood' as its sole basis for determining sanity. Other than confessing to be an angel, Ms. Doe meets the requirements for competency to stand trial."

"Come on, come on," Jake muttered beside her.

"However, the court is also aware that Ms. Doe's name did not appear on the original warrant, an oversight that would certainly be questioned at a trial, as well as the investigating officer's failure to follow up on Ms. Doe's references to an identical address in Illinois, which, thanks to Mr. Stone, has shed a disturbing light on these proceedings. Therefore, I will entertain a motion to drop all charges."

Jake leaped to his feet. "I so move, Your Honor."

"No objection," Sue Cheney said, strangely subdued.

"Then let the record show that all charges have been—"

"No!" Monica cried, leaping to her feet. "Your Honor, I—I don't want to go free." Even as she spoke the words, she was aware of how ridiculous they must sound to everyone in the courtroom.

"What?" Jake screamed at her. "Are you crazy, after all?"

"Maybe. Maybe I am." She couldn't explain. Not here. Not now. These people wouldn't understand. They wouldn't even care. Sometimes an angel has to do what she has to do. This was one of those times. "Your Honor, please, I want to go back to the mental hospital."

The judge looked as if he hadn't heard her right. "Let me get this straight," he said. "You're asking to be committed?"

"Yes, I am. I want to plead crazy."

"Your Honor . . ." Jake began, then turned to Monica. "Why? What are you thinking? Do you understand that you could not be released for fifteen, twenty years? Even longer? What are you doing?"

Monica nodded vehemently. "I understand. This is what I want to do, Your Honor."

Jake covered his face with his hands, his fingers drawing downward slowly in a gesture of disbelief. Even Sue seemed disappointed. Monica looked down. At this moment, they weren't her main concern. Finally, after all this, she was aware of her higher purpose.

A few moments later, it was all over and a guard was handcuffing Monica once again. Everyone was leaving the courtroom, shaking their heads and talking to one another in low tones. Jake picked up a stack of yellow legal pads, four #2 pencils, and his spiral-bound month-at-a-glance calendar and slowly returned them to his briefcase.

"Just a minute," Monica told the guard as she took a step toward Jake. "Jake, remember when I said I was sure I heard Florida, even though it was Illinois?"

Jake wouldn't look at her. "I don't want to hear this," he said.

"Please, Jake, I *did* hear Florida. My ears may have heard Illinois, but my spirit heard Florida. God doesn't make mistakes. I was supposed to be here. But not for you or the man in the bed." She paused. "For Claire."

Jake finally looked up. "Claire?"

"Your Claire is my roommate at the hospital. She's an angel, too, and she needs me now."

He stared at her with wide eyes. "You really are insane," he said slowly.

It didn't matter if Jake believed her. She had finally realized that proving she was an angel to Jake, Sue Cheney, Judge Webster, or anyone else wasn't her mission.

Jake's eyes shot daggers at her. "You were *off*, lady. Free as a bird, and now you're willingly going back to that hellhole. You're throwing your life away."

"There is no greater love than to give your life for a friend. I learned that from Claire. So did you."

Jake didn't answer.

"Thank you for all your help," she said. "Whether you believe it or not, God has used you for something beautiful."

Jake sighed deeply, then nodded as the guard led Monica toward the side door where she stopped to wave to him.

There was only one place to go after a courtroom episode like the one Jake had endured today. It was early, but a stool at The Sidebar seemed to be calling the public defender's name. It was fairly quiet at 3:30 and would be a good place to sit for a while and sift through the day's events. But he'd only been sitting there a short time when he realized he was becoming more depressed. He just couldn't make sense out of any of it, and he was tired of trying. He gulped the last of his drink, laid a ten-dollar bill on the bar, and turned to leave.

But then a deep voice behind him calling out a certain name froze him in his steps.

"Tess? Where have you been?"

"Come on over here and sit down," was the reply.

Jake looked back over his shoulder and saw the man he had met a few days before occupying a stool at the other end of the bar. A jovial woman with an ample frame sat down beside him, and in animated voices they began to converse.

"I've been filling in for Monica." The woman shook her head. "Paris, Cuba, Illinois. How's she doing anyway?"

"You've trained her well, Tess. She just made a tremendous sacrifice."

"Then we're back on track?"

"Turns out she was never off."

"No kidding," Tess exclaimed, looking heavenward. "It would be nice to know these things in advance, if you know what I mean."

Jake started toward them, but right at that moment Sue Cheney appeared at his side.

"Jake! No happy hour jokes, I promise. If anyone deserves a few drinks today, it's you."

"Yeah, thanks, but . . ." He turned back to the bar, but the stools were empty. ". . . but I was just leaving."

And he was out of The Sidebar in a flash.

Pete removed Monica's handcuffs in front of Room 23. She looked in to see Claire coiled on her bed.

"Well, I can't say I'm glad to see you back here," he said as they entered the room, "but I bet Claire is, aren't you, Claire?"

Claire was quiet.

"She hasn't said a word since you left," Pete said.

"When was Claire first committed?" Monica asked. She could guess, but she wanted to make sure she was right.

Pete shrugged. "It was long before my time," he told her. "I guess she was in Viet Nam or something. Part of the last group of P.O.W.s, I think." He shook his head. "It's a sad case," he said as he walked out, leaving the two women alone and the door ajar.

Monica hesitantly approached Claire, knelt beside her bed, and took her hand.

"Mayday," Claire murmured.

"I know all about May Ling," Monica said softly.

Claire raised her head to look Monica square in the face.

"Where is she now?" Monica asked.

"Don't know. Bye-bye, angel." She put up her hands as if to block the memory Monica was trying to force on her.

"I don't know what happened to May Ling either, Claire. And I don't know what you saw in Viet Nam after the Americans left. But I know it's why you're here now."

"So many. Mayday, Mayday, Mayday."

Suddenly something dawned on Monica. "Mayday," she said thoughtfully. "Sometimes they spoke French in Saigon. M'aidez. M'aidez. Help me." Her heart filled with compassion for Claire. "Every child must have been a little Mayday to you."

"I couldn't help them all." Claire's eyes were full of regret. "I failed. I lost Mayday, and God turned His back on me. And now I've forgotten who I am."

"No, that's not true. It's you who have forgotten who God is. He would never turn His back on you. Nothing ... not death or life or war, not the past, the present, or the future, no one, no creature on this earth can ever separate you from God's love. And nobody knows that better than an angel. You are an angel, aren't you, Claire?"

Claire straightened up and squeezed Monica's hand.

"I'm an angel too, Claire," Monica said. "And I've been sent here to take you home. And I'm going to stay right here until you're ready."

Claire began to weep softly. "I can't find my way back to heaven."

"Just reach up," Monica pressed gently. "Just a little. He will take you the rest of the way. I know."

Monica released Claire's hand, and slowly, tentatively, Claire extended her arms upward. A glow of light filled the tiny cell, and then the two angels were garbed in layer upon layer of the brightest white robes. Monica embraced Claire, and they clung to each other for a moment.

"Claire?" a voice spoke from the doorway.

They turned to find Jake standing there, looking awestruck. Claire nodded to him. Then Monica heard the inner voice and looked quickly at Claire. She could tell by the radiant expression on her face that she'd heard it, too. Monica nodded to Claire.

"I have a message for you, Jake," Claire began. "I was supposed to deliver it a long time ago on the helicopter, but I chose to stay behind. God used me anyway to catch May Ling."

Jake looked a little shaky. He walked over to the bed and sat down on the edge. Claire immediately knelt at his feet.

"Jake, oh Jake, God loves you," Claire went on. "And He knows all the secrets of your heart. The horrors of the war you had to endure—you mustn't blame Him for. But you've allowed the past to come between you and God."

Jake bowed his head and wept, then reached out to Claire and clung to her. She caressed his head.

"Turn the past over to God, Jake," she murmured. "He is strong enough to take it. And give Him your future, too. And Jake, He'll make *you* strong enough to live it. I think you have the faith now to try."

Jake nodded but kept his head bowed. When he looked up, he was alone.

Across town Tess and Monica revisited the room where it had all started at 801 Cedar Street. They were surrounded by a ladder, a few cans of paint, some tools, a decorator's color wheel, and a ring of fabric swatches about nine inches thick, and a flat object, wrapped loosely in brown paper.

"It's a state law," Tess said. "They confiscate everything and auction it off."

"I hope the new tenants will be happy here," Monica said, looking around. "And cleaner than the last guy."

"There won't be any new tenants, baby," Tess said. "It's gonna be fixed up and turned into a . . ." She pulled some papers out of a large vinyl tote bag. ". . . a home for orphans and child survivors of trauma."

Monica eagerly took the papers to read the details for herself.

"There's the best part." Tess, looking over Monica's shoulder, pointed to a particular paragraph on page seven. "Executive Director: May Ling Gustafson." The two angels smiled at one another. "Funny how it always works out sooner or later, huh?"

Monica looked hopefully at Tess. "Before we go, can I just make one short stop . . ."

"At Jake's?" Tess waved a hand. "Yes, but then you come straight home, Miss Wings. Straight home!"

"Promise!"

A breeze blew up the lacey white curtain, and a dove landed on the freshly painted sill. A gust of wind then loosened the brown paper from the parcel on the floor to reveal a bronze plaque. It read:

"Dedicated to a man named Jake and an angel named Claire. They served their country, their God, and many children with all they had. May we here do the same." ⟿

Response to the Show

Roma Downey

This was the first episode where my pregnancy was starting to show. Between the wardrobe department and the camera department, we were coming up with all sorts of ways to disguise the ever-growing Reilly Marie. We didn't think America was ready for a pregnant angel.

There are times when the script is written so that the dramatic action falls to the guest star. We've had some very powerful episodes when this has happened. Still, the actor in me doesn't get the challenge that I so love. Among my favorites are the shows where I really have something to sink my teeth into. I think "Jacob's Ladder" was one of those episodes.

FROM VIEWERS

I really relate to the human side of Monica, like when she was in jail in "Jacob's Ladder" or on the street in the episode about the homeless. She felt so abandoned in the mental hospital, and so did the other angel, named Claire. I have often felt that way as well, like God didn't need me and I could no longer be effective with anyone.

Monica didn't expect things to turn out the way they did, but she knew that God had used her mistake to make something beautiful come about. I want to believe that He can also use my life in ways I couldn't anticipate.

Fort Worth, Texas

The episode with Cindy Williams as an angel who forgot or lost her purpose was extra meaningful to us. It was food for much thought and reflection about our own lives as believers. Sometimes we do forget our purpose on earth, then someone comes along "by chance"—more likely by God's hand guiding them to us—to encourage and remind us of our purpose as believers and that God has not forgotten us.

Littleton, Colorado

PART THREE

THE STARS AND THE FANS OF

Touched by an Angel

DELLA ON THE SET OF "WRITTEN IN DUST"

ROMA IN MAKEUP ON THE SET OF "WRITTEN IN DUST"

CHAPTER 6

A WORD FROM ROMA DOWNEY

*R*oma Downey grew up in Derry, Northern Ireland. A classically trained actress who toured with Dublin's renowned Abbey Players, she has performed on and off Broadway and co-starred in the CBS television film *A Child Is Missing* with Henry Winkler. Prior to accepting the role of Monica, she was best-known for her portrayal of Jackie Kennedy in the Emmy-winning television miniseries *A Woman Named Jackie*. The mother of her own little angel—nine-month-old daughter, Reilly Marie—she is married to film director David Anspaugh. They make their home in Salt Lake City, Utah, where the show is filmed.

~

"Mommy, there's the angel!" a small girl exclaimed as we passed each other in a crowded mall. Awestruck, her little face looked as though she, too, had suddenly been "touched by an angel." I couldn't help but smile as those big eyes followed me, desperately hoping I would spread my wings or perform a miracle right there in the middle of the mall.

Whenever something like that happens, I realize what a responsibility it is to play Monica, the angel with the Irish lilt,

on a show that has touched both children and adults.

I remember the letter from a woman whose life was changed by the episode featuring Phylicia Rashad, who played an alcoholic tearfully reconciled to her daughter. That story had given this young woman real-life courage to confront her own alcoholic mother.

Then there was a letter from a prisoner, embittered because he was living behind bars, cut off from his family. A show about a fractured relationship between a father and son motivated him to attempt to make things right with his own son.

One after the other, parents tell me how grateful they are for a series that isn't obsessed with sex and violence. They love to sit down with their families and watch the show without keeping one hand poised over the remote in case an offensive scene pops up. They seem pleased that someone actually dares to say the word *God* respectfully on prime-time TV.

Another unexpected benefit of my angelic role has been working side by side with Della Reese, who plays Tess, my supervising angel. Della has such a motherly touch, something especially precious to me, since my mother died when I was only ten. The love you see on the screen between Tess and Monica is the real thing, I assure you.

In fact, the initial script appealed to me because it portrayed two strong women (angels in this case) who liked each other. It was such a contrast to other roles I'd been asked to consider: girlfriend, lover, wife, secretary. As an actress, you often feel you've been cast as a decorative element, to make the male lead look good. It's difficult to find really strong parts. Since I refused to consider roles that required me to do nude scenes, whether in movies or on TV, that seemed to narrow my choices even more. In *Touched by an Angel* I found a script that felt right, a script where the main characters loved and respected each other.

But finding the script and landing the job were two different things entirely. People tell me my Irish accent is charming, but it's often a liability in the acting profession. The script was originally written for an American Monica, but the producers wanted me to read with my native accent instead of the American voice I had perfected. Though they loved the way I read the part, they told me they had already offered it to a major star. Auditions were a precaution in case she didn't accept.

Fortunately for me, she passed on the role, and I was thrilled to be next in line. Still, I had only landed the lead in a pilot, not a series. I knew as well as anyone that most pilots never made it to prime time. Once CBS bought the original pilot, they hired Martha Williamson as executive producer. Martha completely revamped the script and retooled the show's vision. Still, a lot of people didn't think we'd make it.

We sort of hiccuped our way through the first season, and then the series really caught on. It was a hit even though the media seemed to ignore us. Della and I used to joke about how available we were for interviews. We couldn't figure out why the press wasn't knocking on our doors. I wondered if some journalists had become so cynical that they found the mention of God offensive. But that's beginning to change now that there's so much grassroots enthusiasm for the show.

After our first year on the air, John Dye joined us, playing the role of Andrew, the angel of death. His talents have really filled out our team.

Even though I'm as human as the next person, I enjoy playing the high-flying Monica because, like all of us, she grapples with real-life heartaches and dilemmas. I also find her idiosyncrasies endearing. Her penchant for different kinds of hats, for instance, generates lots of fan mail asking where she gets them all. And people are always sending coffee to satisfy Monica's love affair with caffeine.

The show has become more popular than anyone in the cast would ever have dreamed—anyone besides Della, that is. Despite the odds, she believed it had a great future. But then that's her story. I'll let her tell it. ◅

CHAPTER 7

A WORD FROM DELLA REESE

*D*ella Reese grew up in Detroit, Michigan. As a teenager, she toured with Mahalia Jackson and was the first performer to take gospel music into the casinos of Las Vegas. A vocalist with the Erskine Hawkins Orchestra, she began making her own recordings, with "And That Reminds Me" and "Don't You Know," two of her biggest hits. Her second Grammy nomination was in 1987 as Best Female Soloist in Gospel Music. Her latest album is entitled, "Some of My Best Friends Are the Blues." Over the years she has logged more than twenty appearances on *The Ed Sullivan Show*, played the mother of Mr. T. on *The A-Team*, and made numerous television appearances.

If you had told me a few years ago that I would be starring in a television series about angels, I wouldn't have believed you. It isn't the angels that would have surprised me. (Anyone who started out in the red-light district in Detroit and ended up where I have wouldn't find it that tough to believe in

angels.) What's hard to believe is that I would have broken my self-imposed promise never to do another TV series.

A few years ago, I was working with Red Foxx on a new show. In the middle of it, he collapsed in my arms and died four and a half hours later. I'll never forget the scene in the hospital waiting room. The doctor broke the news as gently as he could to Mrs. Foxx. Without skipping a beat, the show's executives started discussing how they would handle rewrites and who they would get to play the lead. Their anxiety about the show's success apparently overshadowed their sense of common decency. It must have been hard for Mrs. Foxx to accept their condolences—when they were finally offered. That's when I decided to get back on the concert circuit. I didn't want to work in that kind of atmosphere anymore.

When my agent called me about *Touched by an Angel*, he disarmed my fears about doing a TV series: "This is a pilot that won't work, but the check won't bounce." With that, I decided it was safe to go ahead and accept the job. But some people at CBS were more interested in the show than either of us had suspected.

Once the pilot was shot, they brought in Martha Williamson, a new executive producer, to rescue it. I remember meeting with Martha, Roma, and some television executives around a table to discuss the fate of the series. Suddenly, Martha stood up and said: "I just want you to know that this show is going to be about God and we're going to say the word *God*. I want to know if that's all right."

I've been a preacher for nine years and singing gospel since I was six years old, so I didn't mind chiming in: "Yes, Martha, God's all right with me, has been for a long time." Suddenly I had a better feeling about the series. It wasn't going to be this heartless, corporate thing after all.

Later that day, I spent some time praying about things. I sensed God saying: "Do this for Me and you can retire afterwards." From then on I felt sure the show would last another ten years, by which time I will be seventy-five years old. (I'm not saying I'll retire then, but having a little more freedom to do what I'd like would be nice.) I told God I'd be happy to stick with the series for however long He intended. Meanwhile, all those television executives were deliberating about whether to invest in it. I didn't worry because I had already heard it from "The Chairman of the Board," if you know what I mean. I was sure the show would go on.

The network bought six episodes, and everybody was nervous whether we would make it. Because I had the inside track, I kept encouraging folks to hang in there, assuring them we would last ten years. To everyone's relief, the show really took off.

Being part of *Touched by an Angel* has been special for so many reasons. People stop me in airports and supermarkets to tell me how glad they are for something that offers them spiritual food. Many of them tell me it's one of the few shows the entire family watches together.

I am grateful that Martha Williamson is an extremely good writer and that the crew is fantastic to work with. And as for Roma—she and I just hit it off immediately. We never had to work on our relationship, figuring out what makes each other tick, what we like and dislike. The chemistry between us has been great. The camera says it all—Tess and Roma are two angels who like nothing better than teaming up on all kinds of challenging assignments.

Not long ago, while waiting for my husband, I was approached by a five-year-old girl. She had been looking me over from a distance, whispering to her younger sister. Finally she said, "You're Tess, aren't you?"

"Yes, baby, I'm Tess," I replied. I knew that little one might never recognize the name Della Reese. But I was pretty sure she would always remember her encounter with an angel named Tess. And, you know, I wouldn't have it any other way. ⌒

CHAPTER 8

A WORD FROM JOHN DYE

A native of Amory, Mississippi, John Dye made his acting debut as Kurt von Trapp in a high school production of *The Sound of Music* and has been acting ever since. He has starred in feature films such as *Campus Man* and *Perfect Weapon* and television series, including *Tour of Duty* and *Jack's Place* as well as the miniseries *Billionaire's Boys' Club*. He turned down other projects in order to join *Touched by an Angel* in its second season.

~

Not long ago, Roma Downey and I attended a funeral in Salt Lake City together. You should have heard the gasps from those in attendance. It must have seemed bizarre to spot the "Angel of Death" sitting quietly through a memorial service.

Actually, I like the role because death isn't something we talk about much in America. As a nation, we find it difficult to mourn or grieve, labeling tears a sign of weakness. Because of that, Andrew is a rather loud character, helping us face something we would rather ignore. But he does it so positively, assuring us death is not the end of everything but rather the beginning of a different kind of life.

I'll never forget the man who approached me after a very long day on the set. "Thank you," he said, "on behalf of my children. Because of you and the way you play this role they aren't afraid of death anymore. I don't think I could have taught them that as clearly as you did."

How could you not be glad to be part of a show that engenders this kind of response? From the moment I stepped onto the set, I knew something very important, something very special, was happening. Though our success has surprised a lot of people, I don't think it's a coincidence. My mom always says that "coincidence is when God remains anonymous."

Though I don't like the term "family values" because it's too loaded, I do think people appreciate a show that conveys clear values, ones that all of us share. *All* of us. Instead of dividing, *Touched* chooses to unite. I'm very proud of that. I also think the approaching millennium has been a factor in the show's success. People need hope; they need to find ways to draw closer to those they love; they need something to take away their fears. The show does that. We always choose love over fear. The show recognizes that people think. We ask them to consider.

But did I ever envision the success we have enjoyed? Though I expected the show to do well, I am as surprised as anyone about what's happened. Only a handful of the hundreds of pilots that are created ever make it on the air. Of those, probably five percent last a full year. An even smaller percentage break the top ten. How could I not be surprised? Today I found out we had our highest ratings ever: The World Series, *ER*, and *Touched*. This is great! Good company, except that the Braves lost.

However long it lasts, I'm grateful to be part of a show that my own children will be able to watch and enjoy. I'm grateful for the chance to portray death as a promising beginning rather than a dreadful ending and glad to be able to consider the deep questions people are asking as we face the new millennium. It's very exciting.

It's also exciting that Andrew is getting to do "casework"—bridging life and death. Pretty powerful stuff. I'm not just lucky. I'm blessed. ∼

CHAPTER 9

PEOPLE WHO HAVE BEEN TOUCHED BY *TOUCHED BY AN ANGEL*

FROM GUEST STARS

Ed Begley, Jr.

Actor Ed Begley, Jr. starred in the medical drama *St. Elsewhere*, receiving an Emmy nomination during each viewing season. He has numerous television credits and has appeared on Broadway and in feature films including *Batman Forever*. He starred in the episode entitled "Till We Meet Again."

> It was a pleasure to appear on a show that has such a positive impact on prime time. We need more programming of this nature.

Kathie Lee Gifford

Entertainer, businesswoman, wife, and mother, Kathie Lee Gifford is the cohost of the popular morning talk show *LIVE with Regis & Kathie Lee*. She portrayed a surrogate mother in

ROMA, DELLA, & KATHIE LEE
GIFFORD IN "BIRTHMARKS"

the episode entitled "Birthmarks."

I'll never forget two of the longest professional days of my career. The first day being fifteen hours and the second being eighteen hours, all the while doing nothing but crying or giving birth. The amazing thing is, I've never had so much fun in my entire life! Martha, the cast, and the crew were wonderful to work with, and I treasure my memories with them.

Jasmine Guy

Jasmine portrayed Kathleen, a fallen angel, in two episodes, "Sympathy for the Devil" and "Lost and Found." She has appeared in feature films and is best-known for her role on *A Different World*. Other television series include *Melrose Place* and *Talk of the Town*.

Everything was cool until the last scene—the showdown between good and evil. Monica versus Kathleen. Roma versus Jaz. Now in the preceding scenes I knew what to play. It was obvious—my intentions, motivation, and purpose—but I was pretending to be a *person*. Come showdown time I was an *angel*. Hmmm. What exactly does an angel do? Especially a messenger of Satan!

Here comes the philosophical part, the story never told to the audience but only seen in our work. I must say Roma has that angel part down pat. I can almost see wings sprouting from her back. So, to confront her intense force of goodness I drew from all the evils I've seen at work in human nature: insecurity, selfishness, defensiveness, and pain. Then I masked it with a sense of confidence, duty, and humor. Voila! Instant devil.

I realize we are constantly in that battle between good and evil. I remember every showdown I've ever witnessed. I realize how profoundly universal the theme and therefore the appeal of this show. I'm proud to have been a part of its two-year run, even if my angel is so bad.

Valerie Harper

Television audiences met Valerie Harper as the best friend and neighbor of Mary Richards on the long-running *Mary Tyler Moore Show*. She later starred in *Rhoda* and *Valerie* and numerous television and feature films. On *Touched by an Angel* she played the mother of a teenage son accused of a heinous crime in an episode entitled "Flesh and Blood."

The whole set was touched by an angel. It was a wonderful experience, especially being in Salt Lake City with the mountains and fresh air. I loved the feeling of being on location away from Hollywood or New York; it was like the set of a feature film. The script was so good and so was every crew member.

This is not a soft show. The scripts are about crucial human issues and passions. It's a very deep show that Martha is writing, but with a light touch.

During filming I had the weekend off and met a sweet, young lady in a shop at the mall. She was trying to raise money for her choir to take a trip to Washington, D.C. to compete in a national competition. I gave her all the cash I had—five dollars—and she said, "You're an angel." Then I told her I was in Salt Lake City to do *Touched by an Angel*, and she told me it's one of the few shows her parents allow her to watch, because it's so positive.

Her choir was doing everything they could to get to the competition—washing cars, selling cakes, doing chores. To try to help them, the producers invited the choir to sing on the set, where the marvelous crew donated several thousand dollars, and the local press covered the story.

Recently when I came back into town to work on an episode of *Promised Land*, I ran into the same young lady who told me her choir had not only received an additional $20,000 as a result of the news stories, but they won the competition! I'll always remember the warmth of this cast and crew and how they enabled these young people to reach their dream.

Randy Travis

Singer Randy Travis is a favorite of country music fans everywhere. He made special guest star appearances on two Christmas-themed episodes, "Fear Not!" and "The Feather." Travis played a cynical and overprotective older brother of a disabled teen.

I've worked with the cast and crew of *Touched by an Angel* twice and have some great memories and some new friendships that will last the rest of my life. I think the show is an inspiration to everyone who watches. It's the kind of show we need a lot more of on TV.

Joan Van Ark

Joan Van Ark may be best known to television audiences as Valene Ewing on the drama *Knots Landing*, but the versatile actress's stage and voice-over credits are considerable. She costarred with Ed Begley, Jr., playing his sister in the episode "Till We Meet Again."

RANDY TRAVIS IN "FEAR NOT"

I cannot say enough about the show—I talk about it in every interview I do. This is not a sound-bite quote, but I feel such a genuine depth of emotion about this show. . . . Everything is done with such subtlety, humor, and warmth. This coming season it will be "the show" to watch. The kind of spirituality that *Touched by an Angel* offers is a real bellwether for other shows.

I took the script into a conference room, and knowing that Ed Begley, Jr., would play my brother, I was ready to go. After I read the first twenty pages I thought, this is a movie . . . such a powerful story and so well cast. As a person, it was a religious, life-altering experience for me. There is a spirit on this set, and it's wonderful that it isn't filmed in Los Angeles. The feeling of space and solitude feeds the work. It was a very emotional episode, and we needed all the space we could get. Martha Williamson is a strong force of positive energy but never hovers or intimidates. That was an extra grace note.

FROM VIEWERS

Not long ago I watched my first episode of *Touched by an Angel*. I just wanted to let you know you have made a major impact on those that watch from behind prison walls. Each Saturday evening there comes a certain "hush" in this room. Mostly, inmates are society's rejects. Many go years and never hear an "I love you." But each week, I've noticed your scripts always manage to include the message that God loves each of us and we are important to Him. In an entire lifetime of words, goals, and accomplishments, I'm not sure there's any contribution more important. Thanks to people like you and the messages of love, hope, and faith, there will never be enough darkness to put out the light.

Nashville, Tennessee

When I get angry at God I think of Roma Downey's character, Monica, saying, "How can you judge the game if you don't know all the rules?" Although my dad's death hurts a great deal, your show has been a vehicle for God to reach out, put His hand on my shoulder, and remind me He is here for us. Thank you.

Northridge, California

This show takes me to a "sane" place—a place of hope, where in spite of our decaying world of broken homes, dreams, and social pathology, people can still have a sense of possibility and HOPE for the future of mankind. This show deeply touched me and is a reminder of life being all about the choices we make—those of hate and love.

Houston, Texas

I am not gifted with fancy words, but I can tell you that I do encourage my patients, a majority of whom are cancer survivors and/or terminally ill, to watch this great show. Our society has a terminal illness of hopelessness, and this one show above all others brings the message of hope and God's love to all who view it. It is presented in a way that even those that are not believers must believe that there is an alternative to violence and apathy.

No address given

Touched by an Angel
EPISODE CREDITS

FIRST SEASON ───────────────────

EPISODE #101—"THE SOUTHBOUND BUS"

First Airdate: 9/21/94
Written by *Martha Williamson*
Directed by *Jerry J. Jameson*

> **Guest Cast:** Charles Rocket as *Adam*; Linda Hart as *Christine Morrow*; Wendy Phillips as *Ruth Ann Russell*; Mark Metcalf as *Nick Morrow*; T. J. Lowther as *David Morrow*

EPISODE #102—"SHOW ME THE WAY TO GO HOME"

First Airdate: 9/28/94
Written by *Chris Ruppenthal*
Directed by *Tim Bond*

> **Guest Cast:** Charles Rocket as *Adam*; Kevin Dobson as *Coach Earl Rowley*; Linda Gehringer as *Laura Enloe*; Ivan Sergei as *Peter Enloe*; Jarrad Paul as *Dink Whitten*

EPISODE #103—"FALLEN ANGELA"

First Airdate: 10/19/94
Written by *Martha Williamson & Marilyn Osborn*
Directed by *Bruce Kessler*

Guest Cast: Charles Rocket as *Adam*; Nia Peeples as *Angela Evans*; Obba Bahatunde as *Carter Evans*; Rick Rossovich as *Marshall*

EPISODE #104—"TOUGH LOVE"

First Airdate: 10/12/94
Written by *Del Shores*
Directed by *Tim Van Patten*

DELLA, PHYLICIA RASHAD,
& ROMA IN "TOUGH LOVE"

Guest Cast: Phylicia Rashad as *Elizabeth Jessup*; Erica Gimpel as *Sydney*; Donna Bullock as *Anita*; Melissa Lee Andrew as *Beth*

EPISODE #105— "CASSIE'S CHOICE"

First Airdate: 10/26/94
Written by *Dawn Prestwich & Nicole Yorkin*
Directed by *Burt Brinckerhoff*

Guest Cast: Charles Rocket as *Adam*; Susan Ruttan as *Joanne Peters*; Alyson Hannigan as *Cassie Peters*; Rodney Eastman as *Craig*; Murphy Cross as *Lydia Feldman*; Maria Celedonio as *Shannon*

EPISODE #106—"THE HEART OF THE MATTER"

First Airdate: 11/2/94
Written by *Chris Ruppenthal*
Directed by *Max Tash*

Guest Cast: Peter Scolari as *Charles Hibbard*; Wendy Makkena as *Robin Dunwoody*; M. C. Gainey as *Smoky*; Montrose Hagins as *Sister Mary Frances*; Pierrino Mascarino as *Mikal*; Kent Williams as *Oliver MacGregor*

EPISODE #107—"AN UNEXPECTED SNOW"

ED MARINARO IN "AN UNEXPECTED SNOW"

First Airdate: 12/7/94
Written by *Martha Williamson*
Directed by *Timothy Bond*

Guest Cast: Charles Rocket as *Adam*; Ed Marinaro as *Jack*; Nancy Allen as *Megan*; Brooke Adams as *Susana*

EPISODE #108— "MANNY"

First Airdate: 12/14/94
Written by *Dawn Prestwich & Nicole Yorkin*
Directed by *Tim Van Patten*

Guest Cast: Rue McClanahan as *Amelia Bowthorpe Archibald*; Robin Thomas as *Dr. Harrison Archibald IV*; Gail Edwards as *Barbara Archibald*; Jonathan Hernandez as *Manny*

EPISODE #109—"THE HERO"

First Airdate: 3/4/95
Written by *Marilyn Osborn*
Directed by *Max Tash*

RUE MCCLANAHAN IN "MANNY"

Guest Cast: John Amos as *James Mackey*; Bumper Robinson as *Matthew Mackey*; Brian Patrick Clarke as *Coach Mike Johansen*; Bryan Cranston as *Dr. Tom Bryant*; Matthew Kaminsky as *Luke Stevens*

EPISODE #110—"FEAR NOT!"

First Airdate: 12/25/94
Written by *Ken LaZebnik*
Directed by *Tim Van Patten*

Guest Cast: Charles Rocket as *Adam*; Randy Travis as *Wayne*; Rae'Ven Kelly as *Serena*; Paul Wittenburg as *Joey*; Monique Ridge as *Edna*

EPISODE #111—"THERE, BUT FOR THE GRACE OF GOD"

First Airdate: 2/25/95
Teleplay by *Martha Williamson & R. J. Colleary*
Story by *Martha Williamson*
Directed by *Bruce Bilson*

Guest Cast: Gregory Harrison as *Pete Taylor*; Marion Ross as *Sophie*; Malcolm-Jamal Warner as *Zack*; Ken Page as *Ox*; Kathryn Rossetter as *Julie Taylor*; Stephan Gierasch as *Gus*; Francis Martin Linden as *Mrs. Gus*

EPISODE #112—"IN THE NAME OF GOD"

First Airdate: 10/28/95
Written by *Martha Williamson*
Directed by *Tim Van Patten*

> **Guest Cast:** Paul Winfield as *Sam*; John Schneider as *Frank Littleton*; Dick Van Patten as *Jerry*; Talia Balsam as *Dr. Joanne Glassberg*; Craig Wasson as *Tim Porter*; Dinah Witte as *Kerrie Porter*; Donald Witte as *Kevin Porter*

EPISODE #113—"ANGELS ON THE AIR"

First Airdate: 10/21/95
Written by *R. J. Colleary*
Directed by *Bruce Bilson*

> **Guest Cast:** Elizabeth Ashley as *Sandy Latham*; Melissa Joan Hart as *Claire Latham*; Jack Coleman as *Jeff Ritchy*; John Putch as *Todd Barber*; Jimmy Marsden as *Jake*; Jack Black as *Monte*; Lasondra Zarif as *Amy*

SECOND SEASON

EPISODE #201—"SYMPATHY FOR THE DEVIL"

First Airdate: 10/7/95
Written by *R. J. Colleary*
Directed by *Tim Van Patten*

> **Guest Cast:** Jasmine Guy as *Kathleen*; Stacy Keach as *Ty Duncan*; Robert Kelker-Kelly as *Matt Duncan*; Miko Hughes as *Daniel Duncan*; Daryle Singletary as *Himself*; "Eight Second Hero" performed by *Randy Travis*

EPISODE #202—"INTERVIEW WITH AN ANGEL"

First Airdate: 9/23/95
Teleplay by *Martha Williamson*
Story by *Marilyn Osborne & Martha Williamson*
Directed by *Helaine Head*

Guest Cast: Bruce Altman as *Henry*; Gerald McRaney as *Dr. Joe Pachorek*; Marcia Strassman as *Lisa Pachorek*; Dinah Manoff as *Callie Martin*; Steven Culp as *Dr. Rence Patterson*; Jeannetta Arnette as *Dr. Gus Jacobs*; Douglas Roberts as *Ethan Parker*; Stuart Fratkin as *Chris*

EPISODE #203—"THE DRIVER"

First Airdate: 10/14/95
Written by *Glenn Berenbeim*
Directed by *Tim Van Patten*

Guest Cast: Bruce Altman as *Henry*; Diahann Carroll as *Grace Willis*; Vanessa Bell Calloway as *Debra Willis*; John Spencer as *Leo*; James Pickens Jr., as *George*; Steve Vinovich as *Ron Walker*

ROMA & JOE PENNY IN "TRUST"

EPISODE #204—"TRUST"

First Airdate: 9/30/95
Written by *Jule Selbo*
Directed by *Victor Lobl*

Guest Cast: Joe Penny as *Zack Bennett*; Paul Rodriguez as *Ben Rivera*; John Beck as *Captain Meyers*; Barbara Stock as *Jill Bennett*; John Hawkes as *Mason*; Yunoka Doyle as *Mickie*; Earl Billings as *Cueball*

EPISODE #205—"OPERATION SMILE"

First Airdate: 11/11/95
Written by *Glenn Berenbiem
& R. J. Colleary & Martha
Williamson*
Directed by *Nancy Malone*

Guest Cast: Tone Loc as
Albert Turner; Terumi
Matthews as *Ginger*;
Miles Feulner as *Jeremy
Barlow*; Kelsi Copier as
Emily; Jack Magee as
Billy Barlow

THE CAST WITH PANAMANIAN CHIL-
DREN WHO RECEIVED NEEDED
SURGERY FOLLOWING THE FILMING
OF "OPERATION SMILE"

EPISODE #206—"REUNION"

First Airdate: 11/4/95
Written by *Valerie Woods*
Directed by *Victor Lobl*

Guest Cast: Natalie Cole as
Megan Brooks; Maya Angelou
as *Clarice Mitchell*; Michael
Beach as *Sam Mitchell*; Nina
Girvetz as *Catherine
Wentworth*; Michael Flynn as
Howard

ROMA, DELLA, MAYA
ANGELOU, & NATALIE COLE IN
"REUNION." MAYA ANGELOU
WROTE A POEM SPECIFICALLY
FOR THE EPISODE

EPISODE #207—"THE BIG BANG"

First Airdate: 11/25/95
Written by *Ken LaZebnik*
Directed by *Chuck Bowman*

> **Guest Cast:** Jack Scalia as *Max Chamberlain II*; Melora Hardin as *Lizbeth Chamberlain*; Jeffrey R. Nordling as *Jackson Spears*; Lisa Jane Persky as *Alison Craig*; Joel Polis as *Garland Ketter*

EPISODE #208—"UNIDENTIFIED FEMALE"

First Airdate: 12/2/95
Written by *Martha Williamson*
Directed by *Michael Schultz*

> **Guest Cast:** Greg Evigan as *Bill Salisbury*; Brian Bloom as *Clay Martin*; Allison Smith as *Jennifer*; Alanna Ubach as *Cookie*; Brandon Douglas as *Alex Jackson*; Alicia Coppola as *Ava*

EPISODE #209—"THE ONE THAT GOT AWAY"

First Airdate: 1/6/96
Written by *Danna Doyle & Debbie Smith*
Directed by *Victoria Hochberg*

> **Guest Cast:** John Dye as *Andrew*; Susan Diol as *Susan Duplain*; Grant Heslov as *Gale Harper*; Tracy Nelson as *Lisa Magdeleno*; David Newsom as *Mark Monfort*

EPISODE #210—"'TIL WE MEET AGAIN"

First Airdate: 1/13/96
Written by *Martha Williamson*
Directed by *Tim Van Patten*

> **Guest Cast:** John Dye as *Andrew*; Joan Van Ark as *Kim Carpenter*; Ed Begley Jr., as *Chris Carpenter*; Concetta

Tomei as *Kate Carpenter*; Harvey Vernon as *Joe Carpenter*; Priscilla Pointer as *Elizabeth Carpenter*; Hansford Rowe as *Dr. Donald Chappell*

EPISODE #211—"THE FEATHER"

First Airdate: 12/16/95
Teleplay by *Ken LaZebnik & Valerie Woods*
Story by *Valerie Woods & Kenla Zebnik & Robin Sheets*
Directed by *Gene Reynolds*

Guest Cast: Randy Travis as *Wayne*; William R. Moses as *Charles*; Paul Wittenburg as *Joey*; Monique Ridge as *Edna*; Victoria Mallory as *Jackie*; Randy Oglesby as *Pastor Mike*

EPISODE # 212—"ROCK 'N' ROLL DAD"

First Airdate: 1/20/96
Written by *Andrew Smith*
Directed by *Tim Van Patten*

Guest Cast: John Dye as *Andrew*; A. Martinez as *Jon Mateos*; Richard Roundtree as *Murray*; Rosalind Allen as *Evie Mateos*; Ivey Lloyd as *Samantha Mateos*; Spencer Klein as *Dylan Mateos*; Kathleen Sullivan as *Herself*

EPISODE #213—"THE INDIGO ANGEL"

First Airdate: 2/3/96
Written by *Glenn Berenbeim & R. J. Colleary*
Directed by *Jon Andersen*

Guest Cast: John Dye as *Andrew*; Hal Linden as *Sam Brown*; Geoffrey Nauffts as *Zack Brown*; Al Jarreau as *Himself*; B. B. King as *Himself*; Dr. John as *Himself*; Al Hirt as *Himself*

EPISODE #214—"JACOB'S LADDER"

First Airdate: 2/10/96
Teleplay by *Martha Williamson*
Story by *Ken LaZebnik*
Directed by *Michael Schultz*

Guest Cast: Paul Winfield as *Sam*; Cindy Williams as *Claire*; Joe Morton as *Jake Stone*; Barbara Mandrell as *Terry Hayman*; Wanda De Jesus as *Sue Cheney*; Jim Metzler as *Dr. H. C. Arnovitz*

AN ALL-STAR CAST OF MUSICAL GREATS IN "INDIGO ANGEL" TOP: JOHN DYE, AL JARREAU, DR. JOHN, HAL LINDEN, ROMA BOTTOM: AL HIRT, DELLA, B.B. KING

EPISODE #215—"OUT OF THE DARKNESS"

First Airdate: 2/17/96
Written by *R. J. Colleary*
Directed by *Victoria Hochberg*

Guest Cast: Brenda Vaccaro as *Al*; Jane Kaczmarek as *Bonnie Bell*; Brad Whitford as *Steve Bell*; David Morin as *Matthew Tracy*; Ross Malinger as *Jason Bell—age 11*; Tyler Malinger as *Jason Bell—age 6*

EPISODE #216—"LOST AND FOUND"

First Airdate: 2/24/96
Written by *Danna Doyle & Debbie Smith*
Directed by *Bethany Rooney*

Guest Cast: John Dye as *Andrew*; Jasmine Guy as *Kathleen*; Bill Nunn as *Frank Champness*; Clark Gregg as *Don Dudley*

EPISODE #217—"DEAR GOD"

First Airdate: 3/9/96
Written by *Glenn Berenbiem*
Directed by *Tim Van Patten*

ELLIOTT GOULD AS MAX
IN "DEAR GOD"

Guest Cast: Elliott Gould as *Max*; Kelsey Mulrooney as *Tanya Brenner*; Mel Winkler as *Pete*; Willie Garson as *Eddie Brenner*; Patricia Belcher as *Ms. Raphael*; **Note:** John Dye (*Andrew*) becomes a series lead starting with this episode.

EPISODE #218—"PORTRAIT OF MRS. CAMPBELL"

First Airdate: 4/21/96
Written by *Susan Cridland Wick*
Directed by *Victor Lobl*

Guest Cast: Linda Gray as *Marian Campbell*; Gabrielle Carteris as *April Campbell*; Vince Grant as *Lt. Neil Campbell*

JOHN DYE IN "PORTRAIT OF MRS. CAMPBELL"

EPISODE #219—"THE QUALITY OF MERCY"

First Airdate: 4/27/96
Written by *Andrew Smith*
Directed by *Chuck Bowman*

Guest Cast: Ted Shackelford as *Joel Redding*; Marsha Warfield as *Bebe Manero*; Harley Cross as *Marshall Redding*; Stephanie Faracy as *Sally Redding*

EPISODE # 220—"STATUTE OF LIMITATIONS"

First Airdate: 5/18/96
Written by *Danna Doyle & Debbie Smith*
Directed by *Victor Lobl*

Guest Cast: Shanna Reed as *Morgan Bell*; Darlene Cates as *Claudia Bell*; Royana Black as *Teenage Claudia*; Kim Murphy as *Teenage Morgan*; Paul Walker as *Jonathan*

EPISODE #221—"FLESH AND BLOOD"

First Airdate: 5/4/96
Written by *R. J. Colleary*
Directed by *Jon Andersen*

> **Guest Cast:** Sally Jessy Raphael as *Mrs. Angeli*; Valerie Harper as *Kate Prescott*; Anthony Michael Hall as *Thomas Prescott*; Norman Parker as *Leonard Page*; Debra Mooney as *Ms. Shaw*; Denise Dowse as *Judge Caldwell*

EPISODE #222—"BIRTHMARKS"

First Airdate: 5/11/96
Written by *Ken LaZebnik*
Directed by *Peter Hunt*

> **Guest Cast:** Kathie Lee Gifford as *Jolene*; William Daniels as *Whit Russell*; David Naughton as *Michael Russell*; Barbara Alyn Woods as *Penny Russell*

THIRD SEASON ————————————————————

EPISODE #X99 (SPINOFF)—"PROMISED LAND"

First Airdate: 9/15/96
Written by *Martha Williamson*
Directed by *Michael Schultz*

> **Guest Cast:** Gerald McRaney as *Russell Greene*; Celeste Holm as *Hattie Greene*; Wendy Phillips as *Claire Greene*; Austin O'Brien as *Joshua Greene*; Sarah Schaub as *Dinah Greene*; Eddie Karr as *Nathaniel Greene*; Ossie Davis as *Erasmus Jones*; Suzanne Douglas as *Rebecca Cousins*

GERALD MCRANEY & DELLA IN "PROMISED LAND"

EPISODE #301—"SINS OF THE FATHER"

First Airdate: 9/29/96
Written by *Debbie Smith & Danna Doyle*
Directed by *Tim Van Patten*

Guest Cast: Debbie Allen as *Valerie Dixon*; Christopher Darden as *Pastor George*; Carl Lumbly as *Willis Thompson*; Richard Gant as *Johnson*; De'Aundre Bonds as *Luther Dixon*; Robert Ri'chard as *Samuel Dixon*; Norris Young as *Dre*

EPISODE #302—"A JOYFUL NOISE"

First Airdate: 9/21/96
Written by *Katherine Ann Jones*
Directed by *Peter Hunt*

Guest Cast: Olympia Dukakis as *Clara*; Dwight Schultz as *Dr. Adam Litowski*; Jane Sibbett as *Emily Houghton*; Mika Boorem as *Melissa Houghton*

EPISODE #303—"RANDOM ACTS"

First Airdate: 9/22/96
Written by *R. J. Colleary & Martha Williamson*
Directed by *Tim Van Patten*

JOHN RITTER & ROMA IN "RANDOM ACTS"

Guest Cast: John Ritter as *Mike O'Connor*; Aimee Graham as *Danielle Dawson*; Channon Roe as *Lucas Tremaine*; Danté Basco as *Robbie Hawkins*; James Gleason as *Phil Palmer*

EPISODE #304—"WRITTEN IN DUST"

First Airdate: 10/6/96
Teleplay by *Ken LaZebnik*
Story by *Ken LaZebnik & Jack LaZebnik*
Directed by *Peter Hunt*

Guest Cast: Harold Gould as *Sam Moskowitz*; Corey Parker as *Henry Moskowitz*; Russell Means as *Edison*; Adam Beach as *Dillon New Eagle*; Holly Fulger as *Roseanne Fitzgerald-Moskowitz*

EPISODE #305—"SECRET SERVICE"

First Airdate: 10/13/96
Written by *Kathleen McGhee-Anderson*
Directed by *Bethany Rooney*

Guest Cast: Ben Vereen as *Ulysses Dodd*; Roy Thinnes as *Senator Guy Hammond*; Heidi Swedberg as *Marty Dillard*; Jack Conley as *Mr. Phelps*

EPISODE #306—"GROUNDRUSH"

First Airdate: 10/27/96
Teleplay by *Burt Pearl*
Story by *Glenn Berenbeim*
Directed by *Peter Hunt*

Guest Cast: Paul Winfield as *Sam*; Robert Hays as *Scott Walden*; Ashley Crow as *Jocelyn*; Yul Vazquez as *Tony Portino*; Justin Garms as *Jeremy*; Jeff Olson as *Agent Bradford*

EPISODE #307—"THE SKY IS FALLING"

First Airdate: 11/3/96
Written by *Glenn Berenbeim*
Directed by *Victor Lobl*

Guest Cast: Estelle Getty as *Dottie*; Brian Keith as *Leonard Pound*; Allyce Beasley as *Kate Pound*; Ray Buktenica as *Allan Pound*; Sam Gifaldi as *Young Leonard*; Gary Hudson as *Tom Pound*; Scarlett Pomers as *Penny*

ROMA, BEN VEREEN, & JOHN DYE
IN "SECRET SERVICE"

EPISODE #308—"SOMETHING BLUE"

First Airdate: 11/10/96
Written by *Jennifer Wharton & Susan Cridland Wick*
Directed by *Terrence O'Hara*

> **Guest Cast:** Sally Kellerman as *Augusta Abernathy*;
> Richard Gilliland as *Stan Miller*; Linda Kelsey as *Harriet
> Miller*; Brigid Brannagh as *Alison Miller*; Ed Kerr as *Kevin
> Abernathy*; Janet Carroll as *Diana Abernathy*; James
> Karen as *Mark Abernathy*; Holly Fields as *Peggy
> Abernathy*

EPISODE #309—"INTO THE LIGHT"

First Airdate: 11/17/96
Written by *R. J. Colleary*
Directed by *Victor Lobl*

> **Guest Cast:** Kirsten Dunst as *Amy Ann McCoy*; David
> Marciano as *James Block*; Lori Alan as *Rachel Carson Block*

EPISODE #310—"THE HOMECOMING"—PART 1
(Beginning of two-part crossover with *Promised Land*)

First Airdate: 11/24/96
Written by *William Schwartz & Martha Williamson*
Directed by *Peter Hunt*

> **Guest Cast:** Delta Burke as *Julia Fitzgerald*; Ossie Davis
> as *Erasmus Jones*; Katherine LaNasa as *Fran*; Taylor
> Negron as *Chuck*; Roy Fegan as *Jimmy*

EPISODE #311—"THE JOURNALIST"

First Airdate: 12/1/96
Written by *Ken LaZebnik*
Directed by *Tim Van Patten*

> **Guest Cast:** Paul Winfield as *Sam*; Kay Lenz as *Rocky
> McCann*; John Randolph as *Horace Wittenberg*; Peg

Phillips as *Zelda Wittenberg*; Robert Gossett as *Paul Stettling*; Harley Venton as *William McCann*; Kyla Pratt as *Annie*;

EPISODE #312—"THE VIOLIN LESSON"

First Airdate: 12/22/96
Written by *Glenn Berenbeim*
Directed by *Peter Hunt*

Guest Cast: Peter Michael Goetz as *Jordan Du Bois*; Lawrence Monoson as *Tony Du Bois*; Lisa Waltz as *Nora*; Millie Perkins as *Willa Du Bois*; Cameron Finley as *Matthew*

Letters of support for *Touched by an Angel* may be sent to:

Martha Williamson
Executive Producer
CBS/MTM Studios
4024 Radford Avenue
Studio City, CA 91604

Mr. Les Moonves
President CBS Entertainment
c/o Audience Services
524 West 57th Street
New York, NY 10019

Or call the CBS comment line: (213) 852–2200
Or e-mail to address: webangel@angeltouch.com

Touched by an Angel
Web Page address:
http://www.angeltouch.com/webangel

MARTHA WILLIAMSON

*A*s executive producer of the hit drama *Touched by an Angel* and her new series *Promised Land*, Martha Williamson is the first woman to solely executive produce two hour-long dramas simultaneously on network television. She began writing for television in 1984, working on musical-variety programs for Carol Burnett, Joan Rivers, Disney Television, and others, before becoming a staff writer on the long-running comedy series *The Facts of Life*.

Williamson was a producer and writer on the series *The Family Man*, with Gregory Harrison, and on *Jack's Place*, starring Hal Linden. She was also co-executive producer for the acclaimed CBS drama *Under One Roof*, which starred James Earl Jones.

Her awards include the Templeton Prize, the Anti-Defamation League's Deborah Award, the Catholics in Media Associates Award, the Covenant Award, the Excellence in Media Award, the Gabriel Award, and the Swiss American Faith and Values Award.

Williamson is a native of Denver, Colorado, and received her bachelor's degree from Williams College in Williamstown, Massachusetts. She currently resides in the Los Angeles area.

Touched by an Angel™
A Christmas Miracle
Martha Williamson, Executive Producer

*T*his Christmas, enjoy a heartwarming tale of love and trust reborn as three brothers redeem the past and begin a future together as a family. It starts with the older brother, Wayne (played by Randy Travis) learning to love his younger, slightly retarded brother, Joey. Then Charlie steps in, a con man who sets out to steal a fortune from a church, where, unknown to him, his two long-lost brothers are members. As Wayne struggles to forgive Charlie, Joey models unconditional love for an abandoned baby.

In the midst of betrayal and anger, the angels Tess (Della Reese) and Monica (Roma Downey) strive to restore faith in God—and to show Community Park Central Church the true miracle and meaning of Christmas.

From the hit television show, *Touched by an Angel*™, this feature-length video will be sure to inspire you. A perfect Christmas gift!

90-Minute Video
ISBN 0-310-22252-4

We want to hear from you. Please send your comments
about this book to us in care of the address below.
Thank you.

ZondervanPublishingHouse
Grand Rapids, Michigan 49530
http://www.zondervan.com